A MYSTERIOUS CALLER

The phone rang at the Marsten household. Phil answered it, hoping to hear Stevie's voice again. Instead, a female voice he didn't recognize right away spoke to him. "Stevie Lake was at the mall with Bob Harris yesterday. They were sitting together in the back of a restaurant, laughing a lot. They seemed to know each other *quite* well. If I were you, I'd do something . . . *fast.*"

"Who is this?" Phil demanded. The line went dead. He listened to the dial tone for a minute, frowning.

HAYRIDE

BONNIE BRYANT

A BANTAM SKYLARK BOOK®
NEW YORK · TORONTO · LONDON · SYDNEY · AUCKLAND

RL 5, 009–012

HAYRIDE

A Bantam Skylark Book / December 1993

Skylark Books is a registered trademark of Bantam Books,
a division of Bantam Doubleday Dell Publishing Group, Inc.
Registered in U.S. Patent and Trademark Office and elsewhere.

"The Saddle Club" is a trademark of Bonnie Bryant Hiller.
The Saddle Club design / logo, which consists of an inverted
U-shaped design, a riding crop, and a riding hat is a
trademark of Bantam Books.

ISBN 0-553-48145-2

Published simultaneously in the United States and Canada

Bantam Books are published by Bantam Books, a division of Bantam
Doubleday Dell Publishing Group, Inc. Its trademark, consisting of the
words "Bantam Books" and the portrayal of a rooster, is Registered in
U.S. Patent and Trademark Office and in other countries. Marca Regis-
trada. Bantam Books, 1540 Broadway, New York, New York 10036.

PRINTED IN THE UNITED STATES OF AMERICA

CWO   0 9 8 7 6 5 4 3 2 1

I would like to express my special thanks to Caitlin C. Macy for her help in the writing of this book.

CAROLE HANSON SPRANG out of bed. The bright light streaming through her windows told her that it would be a perfectly cloudless day. She glanced at the clock radio on her bedside table: 9:34 A.M. It was a Sunday morning, and Carole had arranged to go trail riding that afternoon with her two best friends, Lisa Atwood and Stevie Lake. She did some quick calculating. They were supposed to hit the trail at noon. If she hurried, it would take under an hour to get dressed, eat breakfast, and get to Pine Hollow, the stable where the girls rode. As long as she got there by eleven, she'd be fine. She could give her horse, Starlight, a special Sunday grooming, go for a ride, and still have plenty of time to help out with afternoon barn chores.

1

Carole and her friends always pitched in at Pine Hollow, partly to help the stable's owner, Max Regnery, but also because they couldn't think of a better way to spend an afternoon than surrounded by horseflesh and horsey people. All three girls loved horses and riding. In fact, they had started a club just for horse-crazy people. It was called The Saddle Club, and the only other requirement for membership was that members had to be willing to help each other out.

As Carole combed her long, black, curly hair, she thought about her two friends. Other than their love for horses, Lisa, Stevie, and Carole were very different, both in looks and personality. That was part of what made it so much fun to belong to The Saddle Club.

Lisa was the oldest in age but the newest rider. She was a total perfectionist who always got straight A's in school. Stevie, on the other hand, was anything but an A-student. She preferred practical jokes to studying, and her grades and sparkling hazel eyes showed it. As for herself, Carole knew her friends sometimes thought she had a split personality. At school she lost homework assignments, stuffed crumpled papers into notebooks, and got caught daydreaming. But as soon as she set foot in the stable, she was all business. Even her father had said that she understood horses better than she understood humans.

A sudden knock on her door interrupted Carole's

musing. "Your POV will be leaving in forty-five minutes," Carole's father announced.

"What's a 'POV'?" Carole asked, poking her head out the door.

"A privately owned vehicle, ma'am," Colonel Hanson replied smartly. Then he confided in a whisper, "In this case, a blue station wagon."

Carole smiled. Translated, her father's announcement meant that she wouldn't have to take the bus to Pine Hollow, as she sometimes did, because he was going to give her a ride. "Yes, sir!" Carole replied, giving him a crisp salute.

The colonel eyed her skeptically. "It appears that the private—er, daughter—is still wearing her nightgown."

"I'll be ready for inspection in two minutes, sir!" Carole promised.

"Okay, honey," Colonel Hanson said, letting his commanding-officer stance lapse. "Pancakes and bacon—if you're hungry, that is," he called back over his shoulder.

Because Colonel Hanson had been in the Marine Corps for so many years, he had a way of adding a military flair to things. Carole loved it when the two of them joked around together. Having such a great father helped make up for the absence of her mother, who had died when Carole was eleven.

Catching a tempting whiff of the bacon frying, Carole quickly pulled off her nightgown and grabbed her riding clothes. Usually she kept everything at Pine Hollow—clothes, boots, etc.—but she had brought stuff home the night before to wash and polish. Everything she needed was laid out on her chair: the old rust breeches she used for every day—she saved her newer buff pair for Pony Club meets and shows—long-sleeved cotton shirt, light sweater, windbreaker, and tall boots. As usual, getting her tight-fitting boots on took several yanks of the boot-pulls. Carole knew, though, that if they slid on easily, they'd probably be too loose for riding.

As soon as she was dressed, she joined her father downstairs at the breakfast table.

"So do I pass?" Carole demanded, turning around for Colonel Hanson to inspect her outfit.

"With flying colors," her father answered. "Here's your reward."

Carole gladly accepted the heaping plate of pancakes and bacon and then dug in hungrily.

"THERE'S SOMETHING I want to talk to you about," Colonel Hanson said as he and Carole drove over to Pine Hollow.

Carole looked up, surprised by her father's stern tone. A quick glance at his profile, however, assured her that his dark eyes were twinkling.

"Ahem." Colonel Hanson cleared his throat. "Some of us may have forgotten that a certain girl's birthday is a week from yesterday, but I, personally, am planning to celebrate, even if it's a party for one."

Carole sighed. It wasn't that she had forgotten her own birthday, it was just that she hadn't come up with any great plans for celebrating it yet. Most of the kids in her class were starting to have boy-girl parties, which was what Carole wanted to do, too. She just wanted her party to be something different and special.

"Well, I had to bring it up," Colonel Hanson continued. "You're so full of boots and spurs and bone spavins that you haven't even been hinting about a party."

"It's not that," Carole said. "It's just that I don't know what I should do." She explained her birthday dilemma to her father. "I can't think of a single kind of party that would truly be fun for everyone," she said.

Colonel Hanson was full of ideas. Unfortunately, most of them seemed more appropriate for five-year-olds. First, he suggested a magician. Carole groaned.

"But you loved it when we got the mysterious Merlin to come and do tricks," her father protested.

"In first grade Merlin was mysterious. Now he'd be more like—embarrassing," Carole explained.

"How 'bout Bozo the Clown—I could get Corporal Gleason to dress up and—"

"Dad, I'm too old for clowns," Carole interrupted. "I'd die if my friends—" Carole stopped midsentence when

5

she heard her father trying unsuccessfully to stifle a laugh.

"Oh, Dad, you're no help," Carole grumbled.

"I'll bet Stevie and Lisa will have some ideas," Colonel Hanson assured her.

"They haven't had any so far," Carole said. The problem was that when she was with her Saddle Club friends, practically all they ever talked or thought about was horses. That was great most of the time, but it wasn't much help when you needed to plan a birthday party.

Carole and her father fell silent. They were both trying to think of a special way to celebrate Carole's birthday. Carole glanced out the window at the rolling countryside of Willow Creek, the small suburb of Washington, D.C., where they lived. They were driving through the most rural part of the town, past fenced acres and farms. Rolls and bales of hay left from the summer dotted the fields.

"I've got it!" Carole cried suddenly.

"What?" her father asked.

"A hayride!" Carole exclaimed. "I can invite lots of friends—even the nonhorsey ones—it'll be perfect, Dad! Absolutely perfect!"

"When we Hansons put our heads together, perfection is usually the result," he said modestly.

Carole grinned. Her father had been almost no help whatsoever, but his heart was surely in the right place.

The rest of the way to Pine Hollow, Carole and her father discussed the birthday plans. They decided Carole would have a party at the house first—her father said it was okay to invite boys as long as there were a couple of adults on hand to chaperon—and then have the hayride. They would serve lots of food, and Carole's friends could bring their favorite CDs for dancing. For the hayride Colonel Hanson planned to ask Mr. Toll, a local farmer, to drive his big hay wagon pulled by his matched pair of Clydesdales. There wouldn't be much time to organize everything and invite people, since Saturday was less than a week away, but the two agreed they could pull it off. They would start late that afternoon, by making lists of everything that had to be done. To give them more time, Colonel Hanson volunteered to pick up Carole at Pine Hollow after the football game he was planning to watch had ended, around four-thirty.

Carole couldn't wait to tell Stevie and Lisa the news. When her father pulled into the lot at Pine Hollow, she gave him a quick hug and fairly leapt out of the car. As she jumped, her sweater snagged on the car door. She tripped and fell to the ground, twisting her ankle as she landed.

"Carole!" Colonel Hanson cried. He got out of the car and rushed to her side.

"I'm fine, Dad," Carole said automatically, not wanting to worry her father. To prove it to herself, she jumped back to her feet. She felt her ankle smart as soon as she stood up. It would probably be okay in about five minutes.

"Are you all right?" her father asked anxiously, helping her to steady herself on her feet. "That was a nasty fall."

For a split second Carole thought about telling her father how much it hurt. Her ankle was throbbing already. But the consequences made her change her mind instantly. She wouldn't get to ride Starlight, or hang out at Pine Hollow, or see Stevie and Lisa, or tell them her birthday plans. She gritted her teeth. No silly fall was going to keep her inside on a gorgeous day like this.

"Really, Dad, I'm fine," she assured her father. She brushed the dirt off her clothes briskly. "Now for heaven's sake, *don't* worry. Get to your game. See you at four-thirty."

"We-ell—all right," Colonel Hanson said uncertainly. "I'll have to trust you. But if you feel one ounce of pain anywhere, you call me, and I'll be right back for you."

"I promise, Dad—I won't ride if it hurts."

After a final reassurance that Carole was all right, Colonel Hanson got back into the station wagon and headed down the driveway. Carole waved and then started in to the barn. As she walked, she noticed that it hurt to put weight on the twisted ankle—the left one. She resolved to put it out of her mind, at least until they had ridden.

When Carole entered the barn, she spotted Stevie and Lisa emerging from the tack room, laden with saddles, bridles, and hard hats.

"Hey, you guys!" Carole called to them, hurrying over to tell them her news. Or at least she tried to hurry—her ankle forced her to limp.

Lisa and Stevie turned and waved. Both of their faces fell when they saw Carole limping.

"Are you okay?" Lisa asked.

Carole shrugged off the question. "Okay? I'm great! And I can't wait to hit the trail."

"If I know my symptoms of lameness, Carole, you're off in the left hind," Stevie said. "And if I know you, you should probably be at home with that foot up on ice, but you didn't want to miss a day at Pine Hollow for a silly little injury. Right?"

"I just tripped and fell getting out of the car," Carole said. "It's really—"

"We know—it's *nothing*," Stevie interrupted her. "Which means you're planning to ignore it, whatever it is."

"Stevie's right—you should probably be at home resting," Lisa chimed in.

"You guys sound like my father!" Carole said. "I'm here to ride. Is anyone coming?"

Lisa and Stevie looked at each other. "Yes," they said in unison, and laughed.

"Great," Carole said, "because I've got something to tell you that will require *lots* of discussion."

"What's it about?" Stevie asked.

"My birthday party—I have the greatest idea for it."

"What?" Stevie prompted.

"Stevie!" Lisa exclaimed. "Let's get going! We'll talk about it after Topside and Barq are ready."

"Fine, but I might die of anticipation while tacking up."

"Meet me at Starlight's stall in five minutes," Carole told them. The girls agreed and went to get ready.

After saddling Topside and Barq, Lisa and Stevie grabbed Starlight's bridle and saddle from the tack room and rushed over to join Carole at Starlight's stall. Starlight was standing quietly as Carole gave his coat a final swipe with a rag. His reddish-brown coat and black mane and tail gleamed in the morning sunlight.

Mocking a tragic actress, Stevie put her hand on her forehead and wailed, "Put an end to my agony, Carole— what's the idea?"

Carole grinned at her friend's theatrics. "A hayride.

I'm going to have a hayride birthday party," she announced.

Judging by Lisa's broad smile and Stevie's whoop of joy, Carole could tell that the rest of The Saddle Club was just as excited as she was.

"LET'S SEE, BESIDES The Saddle Club—including honorary members Phil and A.J., of course—we'll invite everyone our age who rides at Pine Hollow and then maybe a chosen few from your school—oh, and Cam, I mean, he goes without saying—you did say it was going to be coed, didn't you?" Stevie asked.

Carole and Lisa dissolved into giggles. It was just like Stevie to plunge in and start inviting people to another person's party. With anyone else Carole might have minded. But Stevie was so enthusiastic—and besides, all the people she was naming were people that Carole herself had been planning to invite.

Carole managed to stop laughing and answer Stevie's question. "I didn't say, but, yes, it is going to be a boy-girl party. We're going to have dancing, too. So I hope there'll be even numbers of each. I want to kind of pair everyone off."

"That might be hard," Lisa said as the three girls began tacking up Starlight. "So many more girls ride at Pine Hollow than guys."

"And the guys that do—" Carole began.

"Exactly," Stevie said. Lisa nodded. Without her saying it, both Lisa and Stevie knew what Carole meant: It was an agreed fact among the three of them that Max's horses were a lot better looking than most of his male students.

"Well, if I get desperate, I can always ask your brothers, Stevie," Carole teased.

Stevie groaned. Having her three brothers at a party where Phil and she would be together was one of her worst nightmares. Phil Marsten was Stevie's boyfriend. He rode, too, and belonged to Cross County Pony Club. The Saddle Club belonged to Horse Wise. Stevie often saw Phil at mounted and unmounted meetings. But going to a party with him—not to mention the hayride after—would be very special. There was no way she wanted her brothers there to tease, bother, and generally humiliate her beyond belief.

"Just kidding," Carole assured her. "I'd never ruin a romantic evening like that."

Starlight, who was now fully saddled and bridled, nuzzled Carole inquisitively.

"You're right, boy. What are we doing keeping you inside when you're all ready to go?" Carole said. "Let's mount up and get riding." The girls decided to reconvene at the good-luck horseshoe. Touching the horseshoe before riding was a Pine Hollow tradition. No rider who had touched it had ever been seriously injured.

Stevie and Lisa went to get Topside and Barq from their stalls. On their way back out they passed by Starlight's stall again. It was now empty, but in the one next to it, an impatient mare was pawing the floor and pacing back and forth.

"Hey, Garnet, easy does it, girl," Stevie said to the Arabian mare. A dark chestnut face peered hopefully over the door.

"How can she leave her in that stall all day?" Lisa asked. She knew that Garnet's restless movement was a sign of boredom, often exhibited by horses who spent too much time cooped up indoors.

"I guess she couldn't get one of her underlings to exercise her today," Stevie remarked. They each gave Garnet a quick pat.

The "she" that Lisa and Stevie were referring to was Garnet's owner, Veronica diAngelo. She was the one girl at Pine Hollow whom The Saddle Club had given up on liking. Although she rode—and rode fairly well—

she usually did it more for appearances than for love of the sport. In fact, she often bribed, hired, or "allowed" other girls to exercise the mare when she couldn't find the time. She liked being able to tell people she met, especially boys, how much her parents had spent buying Garnet for her. And the diAngelos liked having pictures in their living room of their daughter riding, as all the "best families" in town did.

"Speaking of Veronica, do you think Carole's going to invite *her* to the hayride?" Lisa asked as they led Topside and Barq out to the horseshoe.

"I forgot about her," Stevie said with distaste.

"I guess she should probably come—it's too mean to leave one person out."

"I guess even I have to agree with that," Stevie said.

"Agree with what?" Carole called. She was already mounted and walking Starlight in a businesslike manner. She wanted to teach him that even trail rides required good behavior.

"We were just talking about whether you were really going to invite *everyone* our age from Pine Hollow," Lisa said.

"Oh, you mean, is Veronica invited?" Carole guessed.

Stevie and Lisa nodded, laughing.

"Yeah, I thought about that, and I decided I just can't invite everyone *but* Veronica."

"That's what we think, too," Lisa said.

"Yeah," Stevie echoed. "Anyway, look on the bright side. If you invite her, you don't have to worry about entertainment. She'll put on a horror show all her own."

Carole grinned. "I'll tell Dad to stop worrying. Who needs a clown or a magician when you've got Veronica?"

Lisa and Stevie checked their girths and mounted, and the three girls turned their horses toward the woods. In front Carole set the pace, starting off at a brisk walk.

When they got to the trail entrance, they saw another horse and rider coming in the opposite direction.

"Looks like someone's been out trail riding alone. Max wouldn't like that," Stevie said. Everyone at Pine Hollow knew that it was dangerous to go off by yourself: If you fell, there was no one to get help. "Can you see who it is?" she asked.

"It's Patch, but I don't know who's riding him," replied Carole. Patch was a quiet school horse whom many of the beginners, including Lisa, had started on. Carole politely halted Starlight as the rider approached, and Lisa and Stevie followed suit.

"Oh," Lisa said with a groan. "That's Simon Atherton. No wonder he's out riding alone. He just started at Pine Hollow. I'm sure he doesn't know any better."

"How do you know him?" Carole asked.

"He's in my class at school." Both Lisa and Carole went to the regional public school, but Lisa was a grade ahead. Stevie attended a local private school, Fenton Hall.

Simon grinned as he trotted up to them. "Gosh, Lisa, it's great to see you out here," he said.

"Hello, Simon," Lisa replied flatly. "These are my friends, Carole Hanson and Stephanie—Stevie for short —Lake." She gestured at her friends.

"Gosh, it's great to meet you both," said Simon, still grinning from ear to ear.

Lisa said abruptly, "I guess we'd better keep going. The horses don't seem to like standing here."

Carole and Stevie exchanged grins. It was true Barq, Starlight, and Topside were moving around impatiently, but Lisa knew as well as anyone that it was up to the rider to control her horse at all times and never be controlled. Obviously, Lisa wasn't interested in lingering to chat with Simon.

"Okay, Lisa," Simon said. He nodded in Carole and Stevie's direction. "Nice to meet you. Have a great ride."

"We will. Thanks," Lisa said.

As they started off, Simon called over his shoulder, "See you bright and early, first-period math tomorrow, right?"

"Right!" Lisa yelled. Then she muttered under her breath, "Thanks for reminding me."

Stevie and Carole giggled softly.

"Not your type, huh, Lisa?" Stevie commented to her friend.

Lisa just groaned again.

At that moment they reached a grassy stretch, and Carole urged Starlight into a trot.

They trotted for several minutes until they came to a stream that had to be navigated at a walk. Starlight put up a fuss about crossing it. He was only four years old and could still be silly about some things. He dug his hoof in at the water, but Carole steadied him with her firm seat and hands and made him step into it. After the first step, he was fine. "Good boy," Carole told him several times, patting his neck. It was just as important to praise a young horse as it was to correct his faults, and Starlight seemed to remember praise much better than punishment.

Topside and Barq walked right through the stream, barely even noticing it. They were both old hands—Topside an ex–show horse and Barq an experienced school horse.

When they reached the other side, Carole stayed at a walk so that talk of the party could continue.

"Okay, so who've we got as definites?" Carole asked.

Stevie was eager to reply. "The way I see it, it's the three of us, plus Veronica, Betsy Cavanaugh—she's really gotten nicer since she's been going out with James Spencer—Helen Sanderson, and both Megs—Meg Roberts and Meg Durham from Pine Hollow. Plus maybe Adam Levine—he's not that cute, but he likes Meg Roberts. I mean Meg Durham. And then from school—"

"No," Lisa interrupted. "You mean he likes Meg Roberts. I saw them holding hands at the mall."

"Really?" Carole asked. "Because I heard from Helen's twin brother Tom—the one that used to ride Comanche till he quit—that Meg Roberts told Meg Durham that she—Meg Durham—could have Adam Levine if she wanted because she—Meg Roberts—had met A.J. at a Pony Club meeting and she liked him better."

"Oh, no!" Stevie shook her head. "That's not what happened at all. John O'Brien is in Tom's class, and I heard him tell Adam that Tom was just saying that Meg Roberts liked A.J. because he heard A.J. liked *her*, and Tom wanted to help get them together, so that Tom could ask Meg *Durham* out himself, but of course John has a huge crush on Helen, and Tom keeps getting in the way whenever Adam goes to see Helen, so since Adam is mad at Tom, you can't trust what he says about Meg."

"Durham?"

"No, Roberts."

"Oh."

Carole digested Stevie's information for a moment. "Okay," she said, taking a deep breath. "So how about inviting Meg Roberts and A.J.; *or* Meg Roberts and John, Meg Durham and Tom; *or* Meg Durham and John,

Betsy and James, Adam and Helen. And if John doesn't work out with either of the Megs, why not John and Amy Wilensky? She's always liked him."

"Until Amy found out that John dumped Polly and Jen last summer after going out with both of them at the same time for two weeks," Lisa reminded her.

"True," Carole said, sighing.

"But," Stevie piped up, "*Polly* totally fell in love with him *after* he dumped her and Jen, because she adores anyone who does anything nasty to Jen because of the Peter Schwartz incident."

"Right. So it's *Polly* and John, Meg Roberts and A.J., Meg Durham and Tom, Betsy and James, Adam and Helen, Stevie and Phil, me and Cam and—" Carole paused and looked at Lisa. Although Lisa had occasionally dated—and had almost had a romance with a boy out West—she currently did not have a boyfriend. Stevie and Carole were always careful not to leave her out with boyfriend talk. Lisa didn't seem to worry too much, but Carole thought it would be fun to arrange something for Lisa at the party and have it work out.

"Is there anyone you have in mind, Lisa?" Carole inquired.

"Yeah, this is the perfect opportunity. You can invite someone as your date without his even knowing it," Stevie said.

Lisa thought for a minute.

20

"How about Simon Atherton?" Stevie joked. "He's kind of cute."

"No way!" Lisa said. "Not even if he was the last guy on earth."

"He does *seem* nice," Stevie commented.

"That's because you couldn't actually *see* his nerd pack," Lisa told her.

"Hey, my dad uses a plastic pocket liner!" Stevie declared in mock protest.

"Okay, forget Simon," Carole said. "If Lisa doesn't want him, he's not going to come. Let's think of somebody else."

Lisa paused. It was hard to tell even her best friends about the boy she had a crush on. "Well, if you're really going to set me up with somebody, I think Bob Harris is really cute," she said in a rush.

"You mean the blond Bob Harris who goes to Fenton Hall? The soccer player?" Stevie asked excitedly.

"Yeah," Lisa said with a sigh. "I met him when I came to your house this summer. Alex introduced me."

"That's the one," Stevie said. "Other than the major character flaw of being friends with my twin brother, he seems like a great guy."

"Wonderful. Then it's decided," Carole declared, pleased with the sound of Lisa's choice. "Now we just have to find a way to invite him without being too obvious about it."

"Oh, I'll figure something out," Stevie declared confidently. "I always see him at school. Or Alex might even invite him over to the house, and—" Suddenly Stevie paused. She thought back to the day Lisa had mentioned. She had a nagging feeling in her stomach—something Alex had told her about Bob. "Oh, no!" she said aloud. "I just remembered Bob Harris's other tragic weakness. How could I have forgotten?"

"What?" Lisa and Carole asked in unison.

"His choice in women. He's had a huge crush on Veronica diAngelo for months."

Before the girls could discuss the implications of Stevie's announcement, a flock of starlings flew up from the undergrowth of the trail. Barq and Topside tensed momentarily and then relaxed when they realized what the noise was. Starlight, however, shied violently and tried to bolt. Carole eventually steadied him to a walk, but he kept breaking to a trot and straining against the bit. In a few minutes he was covered in a lathery sweat.

"I think those birds really upset him. He still feels like he wants to take off," Carole said worriedly.

"Why don't you try riding behind?" Stevie suggested.

Carole agreed and halted Starlight on the side of the trail to let Lisa and Stevie pass. Unfortunately, going in back of Barq and Topside seemed to upset Starlight even more. He refused to walk at all, champing on the bit

22

nervously. Like any good rider, Carole knew enough to recognize a losing battle when she saw one.

"If he jogs all the way back, he'll be so hot, it'll take hours to cool him down," she said. "I'm going to get off and walk him for a while. Maybe that'll help."

Stevie and Lisa stopped and waited a few yards down the trail for Carole to dismount. Carole swung her right leg expertly over Starlight's hindquarters and then dropped to the ground. As she landed, her left ankle gave out, and she dropped *all* the way to the ground. She struggled to her feet right away. Now her ankle was throbbing painfully. She tried to step forward but immediately had to grab the near-side stirrup iron to hold herself up.

"Don't you take another step!" cried Lisa. "Come on, Stevie. She needs help."

Stevie and Lisa turned their horses back toward Starlight. After they had hopped off, Lisa took all three pairs of reins while Stevie helped Carole.

"Let's try to get your boot off," Stevie said. "I think I remember learning in Pony Club First Aid that you're supposed to free the injured limb from all constriction." Carole sat down on some rocks at the side of the trail. Stevie grabbed her left heel and gave it a gentle yank. Carole cried out in pain.

"Forget the boot," Lisa instructed. "We've got to get her home."

23

"How? She can't walk," Stevie pointed out.

"Put me back on Starlight," Carole said. "Then I won't have to bear any weight on it."

"Are you sure you don't want me to ride Starlight and you take Topside?" Stevie asked.

"No, he'll be fine once he realizes I'm hurt," Carole predicted confidently.

Instead of giving her a leg up from the ankle, Stevie grabbed Carole's left knee and thrust it up Starlight's side as high as she could. From that position Carole was able to climb on clumsily. She had been right about Starlight: He knew that for some reason Carole needed him to be calm. To Lisa and Stevie's surprise, he quietly walked the mile home between Barq and Topside.

Twenty minutes later The Saddle Club arrived back at Pine Hollow. Lisa volunteered to take Barq and Topside in so that Stevie could untack Starlight and Carole could call home.

"I don't need to call home," Carole protested. "My father's already planning to pick me up. And I'm sure I can manage with Starlight."

"But what about your ankle?" Lisa asked.

"Be reasonable, Carole," Stevie pleaded. "You're *hurt*. You can't walk Starlight if you can barely walk yourself."

Carole had to admit that cooling her horse down would be difficult. Even with the walk home, he was hot and needed to be sponged, scraped, and walked some more. Reluctantly, she handed the reins to Stevie.

25

"You're not going to get rid of me so quickly!" she warned them. "I can still clean tack, you know!"

Carole hobbled into the barn. She went to the tack room, selected a bridle, and got to work with a sponge and saddle soap. Midway through the cleaning, Max poked his head into the tack room.

"Why, Carole," he said, "I'm surprised to find you here. I thought you had to go home or something—I just saw Stevie walking Starlight."

Carole explained the situation, being careful to make light of her injury. The last thing she wanted was for Max to drag her off to a doctor for a minor bruise that she had acquired from sheer clumsiness. Besides, she had been planning a whole afternoon of stable chores. If all she could do was soap some tack, then that was the *least* she was going to do.

Luckily, Max had an adult lesson beginning in five minutes, so he didn't have time to fuss over Carole. He told her to make sure she was okay, then grabbed a few riding crops and left hurriedly.

Sitting on an overturned bucket, Carole got to work on some tack. It was soothing to sponge and oil the well-worn leather. Her foot hardly hurt at all. After cleaning two bridles, she decided to check on Starlight and thank Stevie and Lisa. She limped out to his stall. "Okay, so it hurts a *little* when I stand up," she told herself. "Big deal.

It's not like I fell off or anything." She gritted her teeth as she walked.

By the time she got to Starlight's stall, Lisa had finished putting Barq and Topside away and was helping Stevie. Together they were rubbing him down briskly, one on each side.

"What are you still doing here?" Stevie asked. "I thought you'd be home with your feet up on the couch by now, watching *From Here to Eternity* for the tenth time."

Carole smiled. She often watched war films from the fifties with her father. And like Colonel Hanson, Stevie was a real old-movie buff.

"Oh, I thought I'd clean some tack first. And of course I had to check up on the best horse in the world," Carole answered, punctuating her last words with several pats on Starlight's neck.

"Don't trust us, huh?" Stevie challenged.

Carole gave her horse a once-over. "He looks better than if I'd done him myself," she complimented them.

"He really shines," Lisa said, stepping back to admire her side. "We thought we'd put his sheet on, just in case, since we had to sponge him and everything," she added.

"Good idea," Carole agreed. The sheet would ensure that Starlight did not catch cold as his body temperature continued to drop. She picked up the light cotton-mesh blanket that was hanging over the stall door.

27

"I'll ask Red to take it off when he feeds him tonight," Carole decided. Red was Pine Hollow's head stable hand. Because The Saddle Club almost always made his work easier by helping out around the barn, he never minded doing them a favor. Veronica, on the other hand, expected him and the other stable hands to cater to her every wish, including grooming and tacking up Garnet whenever she rode.

Momentarily forgetting her ankle, Carole took a big step forward to hand the sheet to Lisa. "Ow," she said aloud. She bit her lip, but not before Stevie had seen the grimace of pain that crossed her face.

"Hey, what did you do about your ankle? Did Max take a look at it at least?" Stevie asked.

"He didn't have time. Anyway, I don't want to worry him about such a small thing. He's got enough important stuff on his mind."

"But Carole—" Stevie started to say. Carole cut her off with a shake of her head.

"Can't we talk about something other than my ankle? Like my birthday party—we never finished planning the guest list. So there's the two Sandersons, the two Megs, Adam Levine, Betsy Cavanaugh, James Spencer, A.J. . . ."

Stevie and Lisa looked at each other and shrugged. If Carole was going to insist on ignoring her ankle, they certainly couldn't force her to talk about it. They had learned that, at times like this, it was useless to try to talk sense into her head. "Sure," Stevie said. "Back to the hayride extravaganza. Now, where were we?"

"I think we had established that everyone who's anyone will be there," Lisa joked.

The girls laughed. That was the kind of thing Veronica diAngelo would say about her social events.

"But of course, darling," Stevie said. "No one in their right mind would miss it for the world—*if* they're lucky enough to be invited to such an exclusive event, that is."

Carole giggled. "I hope you're right," she said. "Because if we go to all this work to pair everyone up boy-girl and then the plan backfires, I'm never going to throw another coed party again! I mean, what if only the girls show up?"

Around horses Carole was the most skilled and confident member of The Saddle Club. In fact, Lisa and Stevie frequently turned to her with questions, and she was known for her enthusiastic—if lengthy—responses. But in social matters the roles changed. Carole could be spacey about people, and Lisa tended to be shy around boys, so the two of them looked to Stevie, who had an outgoing personality—not to mention three brothers and a boyfriend. If there was one thing Stevie could do, it was plan a coed party!

To reassure Carole now, Stevie reminded her that all

of the absolute, surefire couples who would definitely still be going out in a week's time would just as definitely come to the party as a pair.

"But who are they?" Carole asked dubiously.

"Tons of them—I mean there's me and Phil, and, uh, you and Cam, and, let's see, hmmm . . . Did I say me and Phil?"

"Yeah, and don't forget about Carole and Cam," Lisa said. The three of them began to giggle. It got louder and louder until, all of a sudden, Carole put a finger to her lips and motioned for them to be quiet.

"What?" Lisa mouthed. Carole pointed to the stall next door. There was a voice coming from Garnet's stall, and it was unmistakably Veronica's. In an impatient whine Veronica was chiding the mare for her performance that day. They could easily hear her through the dividing wall between the two stalls. "Stupid horse. My father spends a fortune on you, and you're just as stubborn as a school horse. What a huge waste of money. I ought to—" Abruptly Veronica fell silent.

The Saddle Club looked at one another. They knew that Veronica had stopped talking because she had realized that they were eavesdropping on her. Which meant only one thing: *She* had had ample opportunity to eavesdrop on *them*. Carole, Lisa, and Stevie all thought back on their conversation for a moment. They let out a collective sigh. Luckily, they hadn't said anything bad

30

about her. They *had* been imitating her, but there was no way she would have noticed that. All they had been discussing was the party. And since they had already decided to invite her to the party, they were completely in the clear.

"Phew," Stevie muttered under her breath. "The last thing I need is a run-in with her today."

"I know," Lisa whispered back. "Good thing she's included in the party—she'd be really upset to hear about it if she weren't."

"Hi, Veronica," Carole said, going out to the aisle. Now was as good a time as any to invite her.

"Oh, hello!" Veronica said, mocking surprise. "I didn't realize you three were here. I guess it's kind of hard to know people are around when they hide in stalls."

"We weren't hiding," Lisa said as she and Stevie joined them. "Carole hurt her ankle and so we're helping her."

"How convenient," Veronica responded. "You can have secret club meetings now and blame it all on a hurt ankle."

Carole took a deep breath, forcing herself to be civil. "Veronica, we were just talking, and I wanted to ask you—"

"It must be *severely* injured for you to be hanging around Pine Hollow all afternoon, as usual."

Stevie rushed to her friend's defense. "She was making sure Starlight was all right—something you probably wouldn't understand," she said.

As Veronica tried to think of a retort, Simon Atherton appeared around the corner. He had changed out of his riding clothes and was on his way out. His face lit up when he saw The Saddle Club.

"Hi, Lisa," he said, giving her a big grin. Then, continuing to look at Lisa, he added, "Hello, Carole, Stephanie."

"Hi, Simon," Stevie said. "How was your ride?"

"Gosh, it was great!" he replied. "Did you have fun, Lisa?"

"Yes," Lisa answered succinctly.

Stevie and Carole exchanged glances, smiling. Simon had obviously fallen for a member of The Saddle Club, and it wasn't hard to tell which one! Simon was looking at Lisa as a loyal hound looks at the huntsman. If Carole and Stevie hadn't already known how she felt about him, they would have expected her to reach over and give him a friendly pat on the head.

"Do you girls always ride together?" Simon inquired.

"A lot of the time," Lisa said. "You see, we—"

Veronica's shrill voice broke into the conversation. "You see, they have to be alone *all* the time in their special little group."

Simon looked confused.

Stevie gave Veronica a withering glance and turned to the new rider. "Simon, have you met Veronica di-Angelo?" she asked.

"Gosh, hello, Veronica. Pleased to meet you." Simon extended a hand. Veronica ignored it.

"Don't worry, Sammy. Even though you're new here, you might get invited to some of the parties for *less* popular people," Veronica told him, her voice laced with sarcasm.

"Uh, that's *Simon*," Simon said.

"Sammy, Simon, whatever," Veronica replied.

Carole had been watching this exchange uncomfortably. She had never been the kind of person to exclude newcomers or kids who weren't in the "popular" crowd, and she resented Veronica's implying that she was. Even if it threw off the girl-boy ratio, she was going to invite Simon Atherton. It was the only fair thing to do, and she knew Lisa would agree. She might not want Simon as her date, but she wouldn't want to see him left out either.

"Simon," Carole said firmly, "I'm having a hayride birthday party next Saturday, and I'd really like you to come."

Simon grinned from ear to ear. "Gosh, Carole, that'd be just swell."

With a meaningful glance in Veronica's direction, Carole added, "I can't guarantee that all the popular

people will be there, but I know all my *friends* will."
Rather than officially invite Veronica right then as well,
Carole decided she would let her words sink in first.
Besides, she was too angry to sound sincere. Veronica
would find out soon enough that, as usual, she had mis-
judged The Saddle Club.

After thanking Carole and reminding Lisa, once
again, that he would see her in first-period math, Simon
went to wait for his ride. The distinctive honk of the
diAngelo Mercedes a few minutes later saved The Saddle Club from having to deal with Veronica anymore—
at least for today. With a final reprimand to Garnet,
Veronica flounced off to the waiting car.

"Saved by the chauffeur!" Stevie cried when she was
out of earshot.

"Could you believe her?" Carole asked. She explained
to Stevie and Lisa why she had decided to invite Simon
on the spot but wait awhile to ask Veronica.

"She knows she's invited anyway," Stevie said. "I'm
sure she heard you mention her name when you were
going over the guest list."

"Actually, I don't know if I did mention her," Carole
said, trying to remember. If she *had*, it was a very strange
way for Veronica to react. Carole pointed out that they'd
better make sure to invite her soon or else risk a full-
scale war breaking out.

Stevie volunteered to mention the party to Veronica

at school the next day, and then Carole could just give her a follow-up call in the evening.

"And I don't mind if Simon comes," Lisa said. "He *is* polite, and it would have been too mean after why Veronica said *not* to invite him."

"Besides, Lisa," Stevie added, a merry glint in her eyes, "it's always good to have a boy around who likes you, even if you don't like him."

"Why?" Lisa asked.

"Simple," Stevie said. "It automatically makes other guys jealous."

Lisa thought for a moment. "Gosh, Stephanie," she said in her best Simon Atherton imitation, "you're right!"

They all laughed. It was good to see Lisa kidding around about what could have been an awkward situation. So far, it looked as if the party would be great. They planned a few more details—including meeting at Carole's on Friday afternoon to decorate.

"Sounds good to me," Stevie said. She glanced at her watch. It was nearly three o'clock. Suddenly she had an idea. "Help me take Starlight's tack back to the tack room, Lisa," she said.

"Oh, let me do it," Carole protested.

"Absolutely not," Lisa said. "You shouldn't even be walking, let alone lugging tack around."

Lisa was surprised that Stevie wanted help carrying a

saddle and a bridle, but she didn't want to make a big deal of it and make Carole feel worse than she already did.

They picked up the tack and left Carole giving Starlight a final once-over.

Inside the tack room Stevie explained her idea. "We have to figure out what to get Carole for her birthday. My mother has an errand at the mall. If we hurry, we can catch a ride with her."

Lisa quickly agreed, and then she and Stevie hastily changed and went to say good-bye to Carole. She was sitting on a hay bale chatting to Starlight, whose ears were pricked up attentively.

"Shouldn't you be going home soon?" Lisa asked.

When Carole hesitated, Stevie exclaimed, "Don't tell me you're going to do more stable chores with that ankle!"

Carole assured them that her father would be there to pick her up in a little while and that she wouldn't do anything strenuous. "It's probably just a bruise—not even worth fussing about. You two go ahead—I mean it," she said, making a waving gesture with her hands to shoo them out.

With their shopping plan in mind, Lisa and Stevie didn't need any more urging than that. They made Carole promise to get her father to look at her ankle and then left to meet Stevie's mother.

After they'd gone, Carole got hesitatingly to her feet. She was thankful to be alone. She didn't want Lisa, Stevie, or anyone to know how much pain she was in— they'd only worry and act overprotective. She was confident that by tomorrow her ankle would be as good as new, and she wasn't about to let anything get in the way of the best birthday party she'd ever planned.

The hardest part, however, was going to be for Carole to convince her father that she was fine. She began walking slowly toward the driveway, forcing herself not to limp.

STEVIE AND LISA eagerly set about looking over the merchandise at the mall. On their way over, they had agreed that the perfect present for Carole would definitely have something to do with horses. The first store they went into was a department store. They checked out the junior clothes department.

"How 'bout this?" Stevie said, holding up a pale pink sweatshirt. "It's got a horse on it."

Lisa looked more closely. "That's a unicorn, not a horse. And Carole might think pink is too feminine for a sweatshirt." Stevie nodded, deferring to the clothes sense Lisa's mother had instilled in her.

They found a T-shirt with lots of little horse heads but decided it wasn't nice enough for a present.

"Let's check out the sale rack in case there's anything good," Lisa suggested. Together they sifted through piles of women's lingerie, fluorescent spandex tights, and dresses in outdated styles.

"Oh!" Lisa gasped. She held up a baby-blue sweater and ran to look at herself in one of the mirrors. "I love it," she called to Stevie. "I just love it."

Stevie looked. It was a beautiful sweater—an angora-knit pullover with three pearl buttons at the neck—not her style, but perfect for Lisa. "It looks great on you. Why don't you get it?"

"I shouldn't." Lisa sighed. It seemed too rash to go running into a store and buy the first thing that she liked —especially when they were supposed to be shopping for Carole. It was the kind of thing Stevie might do, but not logical, sensible Lisa. She put it reluctantly back on the pile.

"At least think about it," Stevie said. She took the sweater off the top of the pile and hid it underneath some socks and underwear. Lisa grinned. "Well, you don't want to *give* it away, do you?" Stevie asked innocently. "C'mon, the quest for the perfect gift continues in Sweet Nothings."

Sweet Nothings was a candy store. It had every kind of chocolate, bonbon, jelly bean, and gummi treat you could imagine. Lisa had a feeling that the quest for the perfect gift was quickly going to turn into a quest for their stomachs.

She was right. They each bought a small bag of gummi bears and some butter crunch. To make it a legitimate stop, they carefully checked for horse-shaped candy. At first they didn't see anything. They were about to leave when Stevie spotted a six-inch trotting horse covered in gold foil.

"You don't think we should give her *that*, do you?" Lisa asked. If a T-shirt wasn't good enough, then a piece of candy wasn't even in the running.

"I guess not," Stevie said. "But I love its shape. And it's made of imported Swiss chocolate." She gazed at the gold horse.

"Do you want to move on?" Lisa asked.

Stevie deliberated a moment longer. "I'm going to buy it for myself," she said. "I can't resist." She took it up to the cash register and paid for it.

"Sometimes you just have to give in to temptation," she told Lisa happily as they strolled on to the next store.

"Most of the time, you mean," said Lisa, munching a piece of butter crunch.

Both girls had high hopes for the store next to Sweet Nothings. It was a tack shop called The Saddlery. It had horsey knickknacks and trinkets as well as saddles, bridles, and equipment.

"If we can't find the perfect gift here, it may not exist," Lisa said. They began to scan the shelves methodically.

"A horse-photograph book?" Lisa asked.

"I think she has that one. How about a new choker?"

"Hers matches her ratcatcher."

"Braided reins? I heard her say she wants them for shows." Stevie turned over the price tag. Eighty dollars. She sighed. "Never mind."

They peered around the shop carefully.

"Look!" Lisa exclaimed.

"They're perfect!" Stevie cried. It was true: All at once they had found the perfect gift. It was a pair of gold horse earrings. They were dangly and had a horse jumping through a horseshoe fence.

Timidly Lisa asked the saleswoman to take them out of the glass case so they could look at them. The gray-haired woman had been watching them in their search. She was very friendly. "Take as long as you want deciding. I've got to help another customer," she said.

Lisa held up the earrings to her earlobes, and together she and Stevie admired them in the mirror. "Really, really nice," Lisa breathed.

Stevie caught sight of the tiny price tag flapping below Lisa's right ear. "Really, really, one hundred and fifty dollars!" she wailed.

"Oh no," Lisa said, dismayed. "They're so *perfect*, and now—"

"They're completely out of the question," Stevie finished for her. Dejectedly, they put the earrings back on the tray they had come from. They were too disheartened to look any further in The Saddlery—everything else would just seem second best.

"You're not going to take them?" the saleswoman asked as they shuffled toward the door.

"No, thank you," Lisa said dully.

They stood outside the store and looked across to the opposite row of shops. Neither pets nor sporting goods sounded promising. But Mama Leone's Pizza had a nice ring to it.

"I think we might need pizza to help us decide a plan of action for finding *another* perfect gift," Stevie said.

"My thoughts exactly," Lisa said.

The enticing smell of the pizza inside the restaurant lifted their dampened spirits somewhat. Stevie ordered a slice with pepperoni, Lisa got a slice with cheese, and they decided to split a soda. They took their trays to the back, where there were a few tables.

Munching earnestly, neither noticed the blond boy waving in their direction until he was standing in front of the table.

"Stevie! Hello! Earth to Stevie Lake!" Distractedly, Lisa and Stevie looked up . . . and into the smiling face of Bob Harris. It took all of ten seconds for Lisa to blush about nine shades of red. Luckily, Stevie rose to the occasion just as fast.

"Bob! Great to see you! How's it going?" she said between mouthfuls.

"It's going well, Stevie. How are you?"

"I'm fine, except we're looking for a birthday present for a friend, and everything's too cheap or too expensive."

"I know the feeling," Bob said. "I remember when I was shopping for my mom's birthday, I couldn't find anything here. I ended up making her a lamp out of a hollowed-out log."

"What a good idea!" Lisa blurted out. Bob glanced at her, looking surprised at her enthusiasm.

"Thanks," he said with a grin. Lisa gulped. She twisted her napkin in her lap. She stared at the grease dripping off her pizza.

"Hey, haven't I met you before?" Bob asked.

"I, uh . . ." Lisa's voice gave out temporarily.

"Of course you know Lisa, Bob!" Stevie said. "Remember, my evil brother introduced you last summer."

"That's right. Of course. I remember you were wearing your riding clothes," Bob said.

Lisa managed a nod. Why was he still standing there? It wasn't surprising that he'd stopped to say hi to Stevie; he was Alex's friend, and besides, everyone liked outgoing Stevie. But wasn't Bob meeting friends here? Why was he alone? Why was he talking to them? Why was he asking her to scooch over so he could sit down?

Stevie kicked Lisa underneath the table.

In a daze Lisa slid over. Bob sat down next to her. Their elbows brushed. By now Lisa was so red that she was surprised no one had called an ambulance. So much for subtly meeting Bob at the party! Her interest in him might as well have been posted on a neon sign.

To her surprise, when she dared to look up from her pizza, Stevie and Bob were chatting away as if the situation were completely normal.

"That's too bad about the earrings," Bob was saying. "They sound nice." Lisa eyed his profile cautiously. It was as nice as she remembered—blond hair brushed carelessly off his face, a straight, longish nose, and brown eyes. Suddenly the brown eyes turned and focused on her. "Some friends are hard to buy for," he said.

"Yes," Lisa managed to croak out. Her throat seemed to have lost all moisture.

"So do you ride at Pine Hollow, too?" Bob asked.

"Yes, I mean, I ride there, I do go riding at Pine Hollow. We went riding there today, didn't we, Stevie?"

Stevie grinned. "Sure, Lisa."

"So you must know Veronica diAngelo," Bob said.

Lisa and Stevie flinched. "We know her," Lisa said. Her stomach turned. She prepared for the worst.

"You know, at school she seemed like such a great girl."

Stevie raised her eyebrows. At Fenton Hall, Veronica was even worse than at Pine Hollow, if that was possible.

"But now . . ." Bob's voice trailed off. He seemed to be debating whether he should talk about Veronica with them. Stevie and Lisa prayed that he would. "But now," he finally went on, "I've had it with her."

Lisa's heart started beating again. "Oh?" she said, copying the innocently interested tone Stevie usually adopted in these circumstances.

"You see, I've been saving up for a mountain bike. My allowance won't cover it, so I decided to baby-sit to make some extra cash. My neighbor has a little boy, a great little kid, and it's been fun. But Veronica acts like it's the funniest thing she's ever heard—that a *boy* would baby-sit." Bob shook his head ruefully. "Last week was the last straw. She comes up to me at practice and says, right in front of the whole soccer team, 'All that baby-sitting hasn't made you too delicate for playing defense?' So of course I've been getting ragged on by the rest of the team and the coach all week. She just *had* to go and try to wreck a good thing."

"What does she know?" Stevie asked.

"Exactly," Bob replied fiercely. "So now I guess I'll know better than to fall for her type," he concluded.

How could Veronica be so obnoxious? Lisa wondered.

She loved the idea that Bob baby-sat. Most guys she knew wouldn't admit to having fun with a little kid. She wanted to tell Bob that she didn't think it was funny at all. Her tongue, however, felt like it was tied in a knot.

Stevie once again took command of the situation. "You know what the best cure for a broken heart is, don't you?" she teased.

Bob shook his head. "What?"

"A good party."

Bob grinned.

"Luckily, our friend Carole—the one whose present we've been shopping for—is having one on Saturday night. And I'm sure she'd love to have you come."

"Really?" Bob said. He looked pleased.

"It's a hayride birthday party," Lisa said.

Bob gave her a big smile. "Sounds fantastic. I'll be there. And now I've got to run, because I have to be at the Appletons' in an hour."

"Have fun," Stevie said.

"Don't worry—it'll be easy tonight. Nicholas has a friend over to keep him occupied." He got up with his tray and headed toward the door. Halfway there he turned around and called back, "Nice to see you again, Lisa!" He flashed them both a crooked grin and was gone.

"Oh, Stevie," Lisa breathed, watching him leave. "Can you believe he baby-sits? How *adorable*!"

"My mother always says it's important for a man to have a job," Stevie pointed out.

"He's perfect," Lisa said with a loud sigh.

"He *is* perfect—perfect for *you*," Stevie told her. "So why the sigh? You heard him: Veronica's completely out of the picture."

"Maybe Veronica," Lisa said. "But what about all the other millions of girls out there?"

"Don't worry, there are only about a hundred at Fenton Hall," Stevie teased Lisa.

Lisa gave her a withering look.

"Anyway," Stevie went on, "he likes *you*, Lisa."

"*Me?*" Lisa fairly shrieked.

"Yes. You. Lisa Atwood of Willow Creek, Virginia," Stevie explained patiently. Lisa's eyes widened. "He kept trying to catch your eye during the whole conversation, but you kept staring at your pizza. I've never seen you so interested in crust before, Lisa. Lisa? Lisa!" Stevie poked her friend.

"Yeah?" Lisa asked dreamily. "Did you say something, Stevie?"

Now it was Stevie's turn to sigh. She knew she'd acted the same way when she first met Phil at riding camp. Stevie would just have to direct Lisa's actions. She definitely couldn't be trusted to think for herself in this state. "I said, we've got to go finish looking for Carole's present. The mall's going to be closing soon."

"Carole's present?" Lisa asked vaguely. "What's wrong with those horse earrings we found?"

"They're one hundred and fifty dollars, that's what's wrong!" Stevie cried in exasperation. "Remember?"

"Oh, right."

Obviously, Lisa wasn't going to be any help. Then Stevie got an idea. She might as well put Lisa's spaced-out condition to good use. "Come on, Lisa," she said. "We'd better go buy you that sweater on sale right now before someone else gets it. You do want to wear it to the party now that Bob's coming, don't you?"

Lisa made an effort to focus her attention on what Stevie was saying. "Oh. Yes. Bob. Sweater. Bob. Right. Yes," she said, obediently following Stevie out of the restaurant.

"STEVIE! IT'S PHIL!" Mrs. Lake called up the stairs to Stevie's bedroom. Stevie slammed her science book shut at the magic words.

"Got it!" she called back, picking up the receiver to the phone in her room and settling back onto her bed.

"Don't talk too long. You've got a lab report due tomorrow!"

Stevie shook her head in disbelief. How could parents think about science of all things when she had a coed hayride birthday party to plan?

"Five days and counting," Phil said by way of greeting. Stevie laughed. She had called him last night after getting home from the mall to invite him to Carole's party.

49

He had told her that he'd be there, and that he'd be counting the days.

"Me, too," Stevie said. "I hope everything worked out with Mr. Toll's Clydesdales. Colonel Hanson was supposed to ask today."

"You've got the Marine Corps on your side. What more could you want?"

"How 'bout the Army, Air Force, and Navy?" Stevie joked.

"I don't know if they could fit in the hay wagon," Phil countered.

Part of the fun of having Phil as a boyfriend was that they could each kid around to their heart's content and still know that, underneath it all, they seriously liked one another.

"Do you know who's going to be there?" Phil asked.

Through Stevie he had met some of the invited guests at Pine Hollow and at Pony Club events, but he didn't expect to know many people. Stevie gave him the list, updating it as best she could.

Phil groaned. "Meg Roberts *and* Meg Durham! I can never remember which is which."

"But it's easy—one's short and the other's tall," Stevie said.

"Yeah, but they both have dark blond hair."

"So do I, Phil Marsten!"

"Yours is different," Phil said. He sounded shy all of a sudden. "Yours is nicer."

Stevie glowed with pleasure. "Thanks," she said.

"And it's a good thing," Phil declared, raising his voice to its normal tone again, "because when we get out there in the open, I want to make sure it's you and not someone else I smother in hay!"

Stevie knew a challenge when she heard one. "You couldn't smother me if you tried! I'd jump on the back of one of those Clydesdales and make him take off!"

"Sure you could stay on—bareback?"

"Why, afraid you couldn't?"

Abruptly Phil changed the subject back to the guest list.

Stevie almost always loved talking with Phil. They were both good riders, and they had a lot in common. Sometimes, though, the two of them could be very competitive, and their joking could get out of hand. They both knew that when that happened, it was time to talk about something else.

They went over who was coming, couple by couple.

"What about Lisa?" Phil asked.

Eagerly Stevie told him about their encounter with Bob Harris in the mall the day before. Phil was glad to hear that Lisa liked someone, especially when Stevie explained that, one, Bob was a great guy, and two, she was almost positive that Bob liked Lisa as well.

51

"So it should be a wonderful night for the entire Saddle Club," Stevie predicted.

"I hope the weather's nice," Phil said.

Stevie agreed. "I know. If the stars are out, it'll be perfect." They both fell silent for a moment, envisioning the late-night ride.

All too soon Mrs. Lake interrupted Stevie's thoughts a second time, this time not so magically. She knocked on the door. "Better say good-bye, dear. You don't want to be up too late finishing your lab report."

Privately, Stevie wouldn't have minded at all staying up all night, if it meant talking to Phil, but she knew her mother wouldn't see the situation quite the same way. Mrs. Lake was a lawyer, and, unlike some mothers, was not of the opinion that rules were made to be broken.

"Just a minute, Mom!" Stevie called.

Phil, who had overheard Mrs. Lake's warning, said that he should probably go, too. "My mother's called me twice already," he confessed. Stevie was glad to hear that he'd been stalling for time to talk to her. Reluctantly but happily they said their good-byes and hung up.

Stevie looked at the unappealing lab notebook that lay open on her desk. Tables and graphs and figures. Yuck. She closed her eyes and lay back on her bed. All at once it was a crisp, starry night. The bells on the harness were jingling. She breathed in the familiar smell of timothy and alfalfa. . . .

"Stevie?"

"Yes, Mom." Stevie sighed resignedly, opened her notebook, and began to write. *"By steadily raising the temperature of the liquid, we discovered . . ."*

CAROLE EASED HER left foot up onto the couch. Her ankle was still throbbing, but now that she'd convinced her father that it was only a minor bruise, she wasn't about to let it bother her. Besides, she was finding that having a birthday party to plan was the best distraction.

Carole looked down at her guest list and made another neat check mark. She'd been calling people for almost two hours. And so far, she noted with satisfaction, it had been a total success. Everyone she had called could come to the party. After the first few calls, it had seemed that everybody already knew about it and was just waiting for an invitation.

There were only two names left to check off. Carole smiled to herself at the circles, doodles, and scrawls around Cam's name. She had saved him for last so she could talk to him the longest. The other name remaining was Veronica diAngelo's. She had tried her several times with no luck. The line had been busy for over an hour. Stevie had probably already asked her in school, but Carole wanted to be sure.

Eagerly Carole dialed Cam's number. A few months ago she'd met Cam while they'd both been competing in a horse show. Before that they had communicated several times on a computer bulletin board. What a surprise it had been to see him in person and discover that Cam was very nice—and very cute. Since then they'd gotten together several times, and she hoped he'd be able to make it to her party.

"Hello?"

"Cam!"

"Carole! How are you?"

"Fine. Cam, I have to tell you—" Unable to contain her excitement any longer, Carole plunged right in and told Cam all about the party.

"That's the most original idea for a party I've ever heard," he said when she had finished.

"So you can come?"

"I can hardly wait."

With the matter of the party aside, Carole and Cam turned to their favorite subject: horses. Without mentioning her ankle—she didn't want to worry him either —Carole told Cam about Starlight acting up on the trail. She knew she could count on Cam to give her thoughtful advice.

"There's a really good book on the subject," Cam said. "It's called *Training the Young Horse for Pleasure and Show*, and it's by Gordon Morse."

"Gordon Morse? He's an expert," Carole commented.

"Exactly. Two-time member of the United States team, et cetera. My instructor recommended the book. Anyway, Morse says that you have to remember that your horse is still young," Cam said. "Going on a trail ride and seeing all those strange things like water and birds can be upsetting for a horse Starlight's age. But the more you expose him to new things, the more used to them he'll get."

Carole agreed. "I think sometimes I forget that he's not an experienced old school horse. He's so good most of the time."

"Well, he should be—he's got a good trainer," Cam said.

Carole smiled into the receiver. Since Cam was a skilled rider and knew as much as she did about horses, a compliment from him meant a lot to her.

"Speaking of experienced horses, how's Duffy?" Carole asked. Duffy was Cam's horse, a handsome chestnut gelding. They had competed successfully in many horse shows together.

"The old boy is doing well," Cam said. "I went for a trail ride yesterday, too, to give him a break from all the drilling we've been doing in our lessons."

Carole suggested a couple of ways that Cam could keep Duffy fresh and interested in flat work. "Try schooling him in a different place from where you usually practice. You know, you can even work on some things on the trail, like making him halt, making him bend around the corners—stuff like that."

They talked for a while longer, comparing notes on riding and training. After a few minutes Carole looked at her watch. She really had to go if she wanted to call Lisa and Stevie and update them about the party.

"So I'll see you Saturday, birthday girl," Cam said enthusiastically. "It'll be nice to meet some more of your friends."

"Friends plus Veronica diAngelo," Carole told him. She quickly explained that she hadn't wanted to leave anyone out—even Veronica.

Cam remembered her from an unmounted Pony Club competition called a know-down. "Friends plus Veronica, then," he said. "No matter who's there, I know we'll have a great time."

Carole felt the same way. As soon as she hung up with Cam, she dialed Stevie's number. She heard Stevie yell, "Five minutes, Mom! I promise!"

"Homework?" Carole asked when Stevie picked up.

"Lab report," Stevie groaned. "But forget that. Who's coming?"

Carole read off the "definitely coming" list. "That just leaves a space for whoever Lisa wants."

"Then I have to inform you right away that Project

Date for Lisa Atwood had been successfully completed," Stevie said triumphantly.

"Already?" Carole asked incredulously. "Who?"

Stevie summed up their trip to the mall and their encounter with Bob Harris, leaving out the shopping for Carole's present and inventing some errands she had had to run for her mother.

"So he's really cute?" Carole wanted to know.

"*Really* cute—and *perfect* for Lisa—friendly but not loud, good grades, and he has a job baby-sitting," Stevie summed up. "Wait till you meet him." They decided to three-way call Lisa so that they could all discuss the party.

Lisa picked up after one ring. "I was hoping it was you guys. What's the news on the party?"

Carole read over the list one more time. "And last, but not least, Robert Harris, date of Lisa Atwood," she concluded.

"Oh, he's not *really* my date. I mean, Stevie's the one who asked him," Lisa said.

"Well, he's certainly not *my* date. And I don't think he's Carole's either, Lisa," Stevie teased. "So I guess you'll just have to take pity on him and *pretend* he's your date—so he doesn't feel left out."

Lisa laughed. "Okay, it's a deal," she said.

Carole told them that she would call Bob to invite him herself and give him directions to her house. "So," she said, "have I mentioned that I think it's going to be a great party?"

"Only about a thousand times," commented Stevie. "Even if it does include Veronica and Simon Atherton."

"Better the two of them than one of them," Lisa pointed out logically. "Who knows? Maybe they'll entertain each other."

When she could control her giggles, Carole mentioned that she hadn't been able to reach Veronica. "You talked to her at school, though, right, Stevie?" she asked.

Stevie thought for a minute. "I know I mentioned the party to Helen Sanderson at lunch today, and I told *her* that Veronica's invited, so I'm sure she knows by now."

Despite Veronica's snooty behavior yesterday, Carole didn't want to hurt her feelings. She tried to think of a surefire way to reach Veronica. "If I can't get through tonight and I don't see her at Pine Hollow tomorrow, I'll leave a note on Garnet's stall door," she decided.

"Good idea," Lisa said.

Stevie wasn't convinced. "If you want to be sure of reaching her, you'd be better off leaving a note at the Ralph Lauren shop at the mall," she joked. "You wouldn't want to leave it someplace where Veronica might have to do some work."

"Now, now," Lisa said. "You're going to have to be nice to her at the party."

"Don't worry—I'll be in such a good mood, I'd be nice to my worst enemy." Stevie paused. "Hey, come to think of it, that's who she is."

They all laughed. For a few minutes Carole forgot about her ankle entirely, she was having so much fun talking about the party. After a while, though, it began to throb insistently. She couldn't even concentrate on what Stevie and Lisa were saying. All she could think of was how much she wanted to get off the phone and go soak it. "I think my dad's waiting to use the phone," she said finally.

"Then Lisa and I will have to matchmake without you," Stevie said.

"You can fill me in at class tomorrow." The three of them had their regular lesson with Max on Tuesday afternoons.

"Deal," Stevie said.

Carole said good-bye and hung up. She felt a little bit bad about fibbing to her best friends, but she didn't want them to worry. Gingerly, she peeled off her left sock. The ankle was swollen and black-and-blue—about twice as large as her right one.

At the back of her mind, Carole knew that she was hurt much worse than she had first thought. But she had too many wonderful things happening to give in to a stupid injury. She refused to let it wreck her birthday. If she told anyone, she might end up with no party at all.

Her father might cancel the hayride, and then she would have to call all her friends and explain. There would be plenty of time to have it examined after the weekend, if it still hurt.

For now, she had wrapped it up in an Ace bandage she had found in the medicine cabinet. Before going to soak it, she decided to make one more call. She looked up Veronica's parents' number—Veronica had her own phone line—and dialed the diAngelo residence. The maid answered.

"I just wanted to make sure Veronica knew she was invited to my party on Saturday night," Carole said. The maid took down the details and promised to leave Veronica a message. There, that was done.

THE PHONE RANG at the Marsten household. Phil answered it, hoping to hear Stevie's voice again. Instead, a female voice he didn't recognize right away spoke to him. "Stevie Lake was at the mall with Bob Harris yesterday. They were sitting together in the back of a restaurant, laughing a lot. They seemed to know each other *quite* well. If I were you, I'd do something . . . *fast.*"

"Who is this?" Phil demanded. The line went dead. He listened to the dial tone for a minute, frowning.

"I'LL GET IT!" Cam grabbed the Nelsons' cordless phone off the wall. "Hello?"

"Carole Hanson has been hanging out at Pine Hollow with a guy from Willow Creek Junior High," a female voice said. Cam had no idea who it was. Confused, he stayed silent. "His name is Simon Atherton," the voice went on. "He's in the class above Carole. They've been spending *a lot* of time together. If I were you, I'd be worried." Cam heard a click, then the line went dead.

The Lakes' phone rang for a third time. Before her mother could complain, Stevie answered it.

"Hi, Stevie."

"Phil?"

"Yeah, it's me again. Listen, Veronica diAngelo just called me, and she's up to no good. . . ."

6

STEVIE FLUNG HER book bag down with a vengeance. She was so steaming mad that she could hardly believe she had made it to lunch period. Her first four classes had passed in an angry blur. After Phil had called her the night before, she'd been *burning* to call Carole and Lisa. Mrs. Lake, however, had had other ideas. She told Stevie that she had already spent way too much time on the phone, and that she'd just have to wait to talk to her friends when she saw them the next day. Homework came first—or at least, Mrs. Lake added sarcastically, fourth. No amount of begging and pleading had changed her mind.

After thinking about Veronica's wicked plans all evening and all morning, Stevie was ready to explode. The

Saddle Club had made a big effort to include her in Carole's party, and Veronica's way of saying thank you was to try to break up Stevie and Phil.

Stevie scanned the lunchroom furiously. She quickly spotted her prey. Veronica was lounging at a table with some of her underlings—the younger girls who tended to flock around her in awe. Stevie strode toward them, her jaw set and her hands clenched.

"Stevie! Wait up!" Stevie spun on her heel so violently that she almost collided with Bob Harris. He had been hurrying to catch up with her.

"Whoa! Where are you going in such a rush?" he asked.

Stevie thought quickly. She could hardly explain last night's events to him. "I could ask you the same thing," she said lightly.

"Fair enough," Bob admitted. "So," he began casually, "that was fun running into you at the mall the other day."

Stevie grinned. Bob Harris did not normally come chasing after her at lunch. She wondered how long it would take him to get around to mentioning Lisa. "Yeah," she said noncommittally. "It's always nice to run into people you know."

"Looked like you and your friend were having a good time," he said.

"We were," Stevie answered.

"It's—it's Lisa, right?" Bob asked. Stevie smiled again. Bob Harris, starting soccer player, did not usually stutter.

"That's right," Stevie said.

"I guess she doesn't go to Fenton Hall, huh?"

"No, she doesn't," Stevie said. She felt the tiniest bit guilty about not volunteering more information about Lisa to Bob, but she knew she had to protect Lisa. If Bob knew that Lisa adored him, he might get scared and back off. Besides, it was fun keeping him at bay!

"She goes to Willow Creek Junior High," Stevie informed him. "It doesn't much matter, though," she added as an afterthought. "She'd be a straight-A student wherever she went."

"Straight A's, huh?"

Stevie nodded. She didn't want to make Lisa sound like a total brain or a geek like Simon Atherton, but she knew that Bob also did very well in school and would probably respect a girl for having good grades.

"So does she have time to go out?" Bob asked.

"Go out?" Stevie asked innocently. This was better than she'd expected: Bob was hinting around to find out if Lisa had a boyfriend!

"You know, socialize," Bob said uncomfortably.

"Oh, sure," Stevie said, pretending to get the hint. "We go to TD's all the time."

"We?" Bob asked nervously.

"Yeah, Lisa, Carole—the girl who's having the party —and I."

"Oh!" Bob relaxed with a loud sigh. "No, I meant— like—well—"

"Yes?"

"Well, does she, say, go to the junior high dances at Willow Creek?"

"I think so," Stevie said. "Doesn't almost everyone?"

Bob said she was probably right. He looked as if he were ready to let Stevie go. Then he squared his shoulders and looked her in the eye. "All right, Stevie, what I mean is, does she go out, socialize, or go to the dances with a particular *guy*?"

Stevie was about to answer when she caught a glimpse of Veronica out of the corner of her eye. Veronica had gotten up from her table and come over toward them. Now she was loitering at the trash can, throwing her garbage out, piece by piece—obviously hoping to overhear something.

Stevie thought fast. "Oh, a guy!" she exclaimed, as if she had just figured out what Bob was asking. "You mean is Lisa interested in a certain *guy*. Let's see. . . ." Bob raised his eyebrows in anticipation. Stevie chose her words carefully. If Veronica thought that Lisa liked Bob, she'd do everything she could to wreck things before they even got started. And just because Bob had laid all his cards on the table, by practically announcing that he liked Lisa, didn't mean that Stevie had to. That would be up to Lisa on Saturday night.

"There is someone—a boy, I mean—who Lisa's been talking about recently," Stevie remarked casually. What she said was true: Lisa *had* been mentioning someone. Bob didn't have to know that the someone was Simon Atherton and that Lisa mentioned him only to say what an annoying pest he was!

For Veronica's benefit, however, Stevie added, "He's a new rider who's just started taking lessons at Pine Hollow. He goes to school with Lisa."

As soon as Veronica heard the description of Simon, she threw her lunch bag into the trash and hurried back to her table. Stevie watched her retreat with satisfaction. Then she turned back to Bob. His face was a mixture of jealousy and disappointment.

To soften the blow, Stevie hastened to add, "It's probably not that serious. I don't think they've been dating or anything."

Bob brightened a bit. "Will he be at the party?" he inquired.

"Oh, yes, he'll be there. He'll definitely be there," Stevie said in as grave a tone as she could muster.

"Well, then so will I," Bob said firmly. He had evidently decided to steel himself against the competition —that is, who he *thought* was the competition. If he only knew! Stevie thought, happy that he *didn't* know, at

least for the time being. And she was even happier that
Veronica didn't know: Now, if she did try to get in the
way, she'd end up helping Lisa instead of hurting her—
by taking Simon off her hands.

Thinking of Veronica's meddling made Stevie remember the goal she'd originally planned to accomplish during lunch period: murdering Veronica. She checked the
time on the lunchroom clock. "I've got to run an errand
before class, Bob," she said.

"But you haven't even eaten lunch," Bob pointed out.

"Some things are more important than my stomach,"
Stevie said, her eyes narrowing as she glanced over at
the table where Veronica and her followers had been
sitting. They were now gathering up their books to go.

Bob followed her stare. He gave her an inquiring look.
"Like what, specifically?" he asked.

Stevie looked to her right and left. "Revenge," she
whispered conspiratorially.

Bob eyed her quizzically. "Revenge. Hmm . . . what
kind of revenge?" Stevie was beginning to like Bob more
and more. Unlike her brothers, who would've made fun
of her, he actually sounded interested in her scheme.

A noisy crowd of students brushed by them. One of
them jostled Stevie rudely. Indignant, Stevie turned to
see who had pushed her. She met Veronica's icy stare.

"Oh, hello, you two," Veronica said, pretending she
had just noticed them.

"Hi, Veronica," Bob said shortly.

Stevie barely managed a nod. Being civil to Veronica wasn't in her plan for the day.

"My, you're spending a lot of time together these days, aren't you?" Veronica asked. Without waiting for an answer, she joined the snickering girls who were waiting for her at the door.

Stevie's hazel eyes flashed with anger. Still, she didn't think she could have given Veronica the tongue-lashing she deserved in front of Bob. She didn't want to embarrass him by dragging him into the middle of it. Luckily, from his expression of disgust, she could tell that he would definitely be on her side.

"I think I'd better leave you to your revenge—whatever it is," Bob said. "I've got a class in about three minutes." He paused. "Hey, tell Lisa I said hi," he added.

"Will do," Stevie said happily.

When he'd dashed off to class, Stevie finally sat down and took out her sandwich. She chewed thoughtfully. Even if she hadn't gotten to tell Veronica exactly what she thought of her and her outrageous phone call, she was glad she had talked with Bob. It looked like Project Party-Date for Lisa was quickly becoming Project Boyfriend for Lisa. Lisa would be beyond thrilled to hear the news. Stevie could wait till after school to talk to Veronica at Pine Hollow.

Actually, Stevie thought, Veronica deserved a lot

worse than a tongue-lashing. If only there truly were some way to give her a taste of her own medicine. Then Stevie began to get an idea. It was a very Stevie-like idea. It was perfect! The groundwork had already been laid, thanks to Veronica's eavesdropping. Excitedly, Stevie gobbled up her sandwich. She couldn't wait to finish lunch and start planning her *new* project: Project Revenge!

CAROLE LIMPED AS quickly as she could into the locker area at Pine Hollow. She wanted plenty of time to get dressed. She was afraid that it might take a while to get her boot on over her swollen ankle. She pulled off her khaki school pants and yanked her breeches on. Sitting down on the bench, she inserted a boot-pull on either side of her boot and began working her foot slowly down the boot leg.

After a couple of minutes—with no luck getting the boot on—she heard Stevie and Lisa chattering loudly. They burst around the corner, all smiles.

"And *then* he wanted to know if you ever went to the dances!" Stevie cried jubilantly. "And *then* he asked if you went with anyone special!"

"I take it you saw Bob Harris at school?" Carole guessed.

"Saw him, talked to him, and made him jealous!" Stevie giggled. "He now thinks Simon Atherton is his competition for Lisa! And *Veronica* thinks Lisa's after Simon, too."

Lisa shook her head, smiling. "Stevie, you shouldn't have," she said. Then she added, with an impish, Stevie-like grin, "But since you did, I won't complain."

"Exactly," Stevie said. "Hey, how about TD's after the lesson for final party plans?"

"Good idea," Lisa said.

Carole paused, thinking about her ankle. Then she said determinedly, "Count me in."

While they were talking, Lisa and Stevie had begun changing. Carole, meanwhile, tugged at her boot, hoping she didn't look too conspicuous. She had gotten it about halfway on, but now it was stuck at the ankle. She gave the boot-pulls a hard yank. "Ow!" In spite of herself, Carole cried out in pain. Stevie and Lisa turned to see tears welling up in their friend's eyes.

"Your ankle's too swollen to get your boot on, isn't it?" Lisa guessed.

Carole nodded. All of a sudden her ankle hurt too much not to tell the truth. She picked her left foot up and placed it gingerly on the bench in front of her. Lisa went to her side and helped her pull the boot off. Carole's sock slid off with it. Lisa gasped when she saw how black-and-blue the ankle had become.

"That's it," Stevie said decisively. "You aren't going to force a boot on over *that* ankle."

"But what about our lesson?" Carole said. "I really have to ride Starlight—he needs schooling this week after acting up so much on Sunday. And what about my birthday party?"

Lisa put a motherly arm around Carole's shoulder. She knew how hard it was for her friend to face not riding— even for a few days or a week. "Look, if you can't get a boot on, there's no way you can ride. A tiny vacation isn't going to affect Starlight's training in the long run."

"That's right," Stevie agreed. "He'll be just as eager to learn next week as he is today. And next week you'll be able to train him. You can't do anything with that foot but rest."

"And we won't go to TD's without you," Lisa added generously. "We'll finish planning for the party over the phone."

Reluctantly, Carole gave in to her friends. She knew they were right. If only she could have managed to keep going till after the party, she thought dejectedly. Now there might not be any party planning to finish. What would her father say about her injury?

As if she'd been following her thoughts, Lisa said, "I'll

go call your dad and have him pick you up." As she turned to go, Max's voice came over the PA system.

"Riders in the afternoon lesson, assemble by the mounting block in twenty minutes."

Stevie and Lisa looked at each other. Twenty minutes was barely enough time to get themselves and their horses ready.

Carole knew from experience exactly what the look meant. "You two go on," she said. "I'm not going to let you stay here and be late for no good reason. I'm perfectly capable of calling my father."

Lisa and Stevie made her promise that she would go straight home. They each gave her a hug and dashed off to get their horses. Carole was glad to see them go. She didn't want them to miss their lesson because they were making up for her mistake: She should have called home the first time they had told her to.

Slowly Carole walked to the phone in Mrs. Reg's office, which riders could use in an emergency. This qualified, Carole guessed. She dialed her home number. It rang several times. Her father finally picked up, confessing to having fallen asleep over some desk work. Carole sheepishly explained that her ankle—which she had said was completely fine—actually hurt a lot. Full of concern, Colonel Hanson told her to stay right where she was. He would be over as soon as possible and would take her to the doctor's. With a sigh of relief that everything was out in the open, Carole settled down on the tack-room couch to wait. Then she caught sight of a bar of saddle soap. . . .

As STEVIE HURRIEDLY groomed Topside and tacked him up for class, she realized she hadn't even told Carole about Veronica's call to Phil. There was no time to do it now. Max hated lateness almost as much as he hated riders talking in class. Luckily she and Lisa arrived at the ring just as he was beginning to explain the focus of the day's lesson.

"Does Topside look okay?" Stevie whispered to Lisa as they approached the group.

"Just don't pat him anymore! Every time you touch him, a huge cloud of dust flies up!"

Stevie bit her lip to keep from giggling. She tried to concentrate on what Max was saying.

". . . so when something's not working, don't keep doing it the same way. Figure out what's wrong. You've got to be able to tell when something's your fault for not giving the correct aids, or on the other hand, when your horse is simply ignoring you because it's easier for him."

Veronica put her brown-gloved hand in the air and waved it to get Max's attention. "What about when both of you are doing everything right?" she asked sweetly.

Max sighed. "It's so rare for a horse and rider to be

doing everything right that I don't think any of us have to worry about it."

"But, Lisa," Stevie whispered to Lisa, imitating Veronica's whine, "if my father spends enough money, doesn't that automatically mean that I'll be perfect?"

"What was that you were saying, Stephanie?" a voice behind them asked.

Stevie and Lisa whirled around. "Gosh, Lisa, Stephanie, I didn't mean to scare you," a blushing Simon Atherton said. "Boy, am I excited to be in class with you two. I guess that means we'll ride together all the time, huh?"

Now it was Lisa's turn to sigh. "I guess we will, Simon," she said, turning to mount Barq.

"Here, let me pull down your other stirrup for you," Simon said. He grabbed for the outside stirrup, but Barq laid his ears back and sidled away.

Stevie laughed. Lisa and Barq were obviously in agreement.

"That's okay, Simon, I've got it," Lisa said. Before he could object, she had swung neatly up into the saddle and ridden away.

Simon stared after her, mouth open.

"Pretty impressive, huh?" Stevie said, her eyes dancing merrily.

"That was the best mounting job I've ever seen," he

said breathlessly. He turned to Patch and began sorting out his reins, half-dazed.

Wanting to catch up with Lisa, Stevie mounted quickly and urged Topside after Barq. Before she could reach her, however, Max began the class for real. "No need to hurry, Stevie," he said. "Remember to always walk your horse quietly for several minutes to relax him and yourself."

Stevie stiffened her shoulders grimly. Of course she knew that you should always start riding at a walk—any two-year-old knew that much! *And* she knew that Max knew that she knew—which meant that he also knew that she'd been trying to catch up with Lisa. And they *both* knew that talking was forbidden in class. So Stevie's only option was to ask Topside to walk. Resignedly, she tightened the reins and sat deeply in the saddle. A glance in Max's direction confirmed her suspicions: He was grinning.

Simon had more luck. By the time he got on, Lisa had completed one circle of the ring. "Hey, wait up, Lisa," Simon called. Nudging Patch over toward Barq, he began to chat animatedly. "So here I am with you, Stephanie, Veronica—all the good riders—"

"We're not supposed to talk in class, Simon," Lisa said, cutting him off. If she couldn't keep him from talking to her, maybe Max's rules would.

76

"Gosh, I was so excited, I forgot! I'll just follow you and try to watch you so I can improve."

Lisa shrugged. She couldn't just tell Simon to get lost. Another Pine Hollow tradition was for the better riders to help those less experienced. And because the classes were usually divided by age and not ability, riders of all levels often rode together. Lisa had been riding only about a year, but she was a dedicated student and had learned quickly. Beside her, Simon looked like the stark beginner he was.

Still, Lisa thought suddenly, she might be able to shake him *and* teach him something at the same time. "I'm going to practice halting," she said. "Make sure you keep Patch walking—don't let him just copy Barq."

"Gosh, I'll try, Lisa," Simon said, concentrating hard.

Lisa asked Barq to halt. He stopped squarely. Patch stopped beside Barq, ignoring Simon's feeble kicks.

"Not bad, Lisa," Max said, coming over toward her. Lisa smiled at Max's words. He rarely gave compliments, so any word of praise was precious. "I'm glad to see you two are paired up. I didn't know if you heard me say to find partners." He nodded to Lisa. "It will be good for Simon to ride beside you."

Partner? Pairs? Lisa groaned inwardly. She *hadn't* heard Max say anything about riding in twos. If she had, she would have galloped pell-mell toward Topside. Now she was stuck with Simon Atherton for the entire lesson!

As Max walked away, she gave Simon a cold look. "I usually ride with Stevie when we do pairs," she said. She knew she was being mean, but couldn't he take a hint and leave her alone?

"Gosh, it's too bad Stephanie already found a partner, then," Simon said sympathetically.

Lisa glanced around the ring. Poor Stevie! Left without Lisa or Carole to pair up with, she had ended up having to ride next to Veronica. She looked even less enthused than Lisa. She was staring stonily ahead to avoid all conversation with Veronica.

Garnet didn't look too happy either. She was laying her ears back and twitching her tail. When Max called for a trot, the mare jerked her head up and down. Veronica tried to keep her even with Topside, but she kept slowing and trying to walk.

In a fury Veronica dropped the reins on Garnet's neck and threw her hands up. "Max!" she yelled. "Something's wrong with her! She can beat Topside any day, and now she's not even keeping up."

Max looked at her reproachfully. He frowned on any kind of outburst while mounted.

"What? Why are you staring at me?" Veronica cried, indignant. "It's not my fault!"

Max ordered the rest of the class to keep trotting in

pairs. Then he had Veronica come to the center of the ring and trot in a small circle. After a few times around, Max said, "Veronica, this time you happen to be right. It's *not* your fault."

"See!" Veronica cried. "She's misbehaving, isn't she?"

"She may be misbehaving, but you haven't figured out the reason why—Garnet's lame in the right fore. She throws her head up when she steps on that foot to take the weight off it. It's really hurting her."

"So what am I supposed to do?" Veronica asked, full of self-pity.

"Dismount at once and call Judy," Max said flatly. Judy Barker was the local vet. She was often called to Pine Hollow to do everything from birth a foal to give routine shots.

Veronica jumped off and led Garnet back into the barn. "Poor thing, I hope my baby's not hurt badly," she said loudly.

"Veronica, if you need any help after class, just tell me!" Simon yelled after her.

"All right, enough," Max called. "I guess we'll have to abandon the pairs work for today. There's no longer an even number."

Stevie gave Lisa the thumbs-up sign. No more pairs meant no more Simon Atherton. Veronica had actually done them a favor—or at least Garnet had.

"Okay, everyone separate and pick up a trot," Max

barked. "Like you were supposed to be doing this whole time instead of talking with each other."

"OH, MY ACHING thighs," Stevie said as she and Lisa carried their tack to the tack room. Max had decided to substitute the pairs work with riding without stirrups for half an hour.

"I may be bowlegged for life," Lisa agreed. They had untacked and groomed Barq and Topside and were planning to relax for a few minutes. They put the tack back on its racks and gulped down the remains of the sodas—another Pine Hollow ritual—that everyone got after lessons.

"Wow," Stevie said, glancing at the saddles near hers. "Starlight's saddle makes mine look a prairie dust storm."

"I'll bet Carole polished it while she waited," Lisa said.

"No doubt. Hey, let's check on Starlight and see how he's doing."

The two girls walked out to the gelding's stall. On the way they said hello to Judy Barker, who was examining Garnet. Simon Atherton was holding Garnet's lead. Veronica looked on from a slight distance.

"Guess she's found a new volunteer," Stevie muttered.

Starlight was munching his afternoon hay contentedly. He pricked up his ears as they approached. Lisa fed him a carrot she had nabbed from the grain room while Stevie went into the stall and checked him over.

"Looks fine to me," she said.

Judy Barker poked her head out of Garnet's stall. "Wish I could say the same for Garnet, but I'm afraid she's got a bruised sole."

"It's no wonder," Veronica said. "Red O'Malley was riding her outside the ring. I'm sure he let her step on sharp stones. Poor baby." She flung her arms around Garnet's neck.

Stevie couldn't let her get away with blaming Red. "Actually, Veronica, if you'll remember, you were the one who insisted on trotting down the driveway last week, and there are a lot more stones there than on the grass beside the ring. And if you'd exercise your own horse for a change—"

"Who cares whose fault it is!" Veronica snapped. "The only thing that matters is that I'm not going to be able to ride!"

"That's right. Two weeks' vacation while the bruise heals," Judy said pleasantly. "You're lucky it's not worse."

"Two weeks!" Veronica wailed. "What am I supposed to do for two weeks?"

"Well, you could brush up on Pony Club horsemanship, starting with the various lamenesses," Judy suggested.

Veronica smiled weakly. "Sure—I guess I could," she said.

"I hate to vet and run, folks, but I've got to go tube-worm a barn of two-year-old Thoroughbreds at the track," Judy explained. She bade them all good-bye and hurried off to her truck.

Once she had gone, Veronica pouted in earnest. "Two weeks! What a waste!"

Simon patted her shoulder. "Gosh, Veronica, don't be upset. I'm sorry about Garnet."

Veronica softened her tone. "Thanks, Simon. If you want, you can put her away for me."

"Sure thing, Veronica," he said. "I'll do anything to help such a devoted rider."

Veronica looked pointedly at Lisa and Stevie. "It's so nice having *friends* around here to help me out."

"I'm sure it is," Lisa said. She and Stevie turned to go.

As they walked past Garnet's stall, Simon yelled, "Hey, you guys aren't leaving yet, are you?" When they nodded, Simon looked disappointed. "Aw, too bad, too bad. I guess we'll just have to wait till first-period math to see each other again, huh, Lisa?"

"I guess so," Lisa said, forcing herself to be polite.

Veronica immediately broke into the conversation. "Simon, I've got something else you can do for me. I—"

" 'Bye, Lisa!" Simon called after them.

Once they were out of sight, Lisa and Stevie burst

into laughter. "You know, we really ought to straighten Simon out about the real Veronica," Lisa said.

"You mean the devoted rider?" Stevie asked, grinning.

"I mean the devoted mall shopper!" Lisa said. "We should tell him what she's really like."

"Let's hold off on that particular explanation," Stevie said mysteriously. "I just may have an idea." Then she told Lisa all about the idea she'd come up with at lunchtime that day.

8

"EASY DOES IT. Watch that ankle." Colonel Hanson helped Carole lower herself into the front seat of the sedan. Then he took the crutches from her and tucked them into the backseat. Once she was all settled, he closed the door firmly and got in on the driver's side. He started the engine and pulled slowly out of the Quantico Military Base Hospital parking lot.

Carole stared out the window glumly. Usually she liked going onto the base with her father. It was fun to watch the enlisted men and women marching in formation. Today she hardly noticed them. She kept hearing Dr. Curtis's diagnosis echo in her mind: sprained ankle. Treatment: soaking and rest. No riding for two weeks.

Keep walking to a minimum, and use crutches to keep the weight off.

"How does it feel, honey?" Colonel Hanson asked gently.

"A little better," Carole said. She made an effort to smile. It seemed as if her father felt worse than she did about her ankle.

"Good thing it's wrapped so well," he joked. They both laughed. Dr. Curtis had tried to explain to Carole how she should wrap the Ace bandage, but she already knew how. "It's just not that different from bandaging a horse's leg," she had told him honestly.

"I'm sorry, honey," Colonel Hanson said.

"It's okay."

"We're still going to make your party the best hayride birthday ever, you know."

Luckily, Carole could still have the party. She wouldn't be able to dance—so much for the slow dance with Cam she'd been imagining—but Dr. Curtis had said she could go on the hayride if she promised to sit still. What else was she going to do? Carole wondered. Stand up and hop around on her left ankle? She had to admit that it was still quite painful, even with the Ace bandage on.

"We'll put our heads together one more time and think up sitting-down games for people who don't want to dance," Colonel Hanson said.

Carole *was* still excited about the party, of course, but even it wouldn't make up for two whole weeks without riding. Carole had been riding for as long as she could remember. The only time she'd taken more than a day or two off was after the tragic death of one of her favorite horses, Cobalt. And not riding had just made her more miserable. Besides, even if she could handle it, she wasn't sure Starlight could.

"He'll be higher than a kite after two weeks off," Carole said, voicing her thoughts.

Colonel Hanson reminded her that there were other people at Pine Hollow who could exercise Starlight for her. Carole nodded, but it was hard to think of the right person. Red and Max were far too busy. Lisa was too inexperienced. Maybe she would ask Stevie to take him out once or twice if she wasn't too busy with Topside.

When Carole and her father got home, the phone was ringing. "Why did the horse make friends with the cow next door?" she heard her father say as she limped into the kitchen. A dumb joke could only mean that he had an appreciative audience on the other end of the line. And, as far as Carole knew, Stevie was the only person who fit that qualification.

"Because he wanted to be a good neigh-eigh-eighbor!" Colonel Hanson finished. He handed the receiver to Carole. "I really got her that time," he said.

Carole took the phone from her chuckling father. "I was just going to call you," she said.

"Good, because I've been trying to call you for the past hour."

"What's up?"

To make sure she didn't forget, Stevie told Carole right away all about Veronica's phone call to Phil. Carole agreed that this latest incident might be the most revolting crime Veronica had ever committed against The Saddle Club. Then Stevie filled Carole in on the lesson—Simon following Lisa around, Garnet being lame, Veronica freaking out as usual.

"How bad is the bruise?" Carole asked.

Stevie grinned into the receiver. Of course Carole was more concerned about Garnet than about any of the humans involved. Her heart always went to horses first.

"Not too bad, but Judy says she needs two weeks off."

"Just like me," Carole said. She told Stevie that her ankle was really sprained and that, as far as riding went, she was literally "grounded" for the next two weeks. "I'm really worried about Starlight's training," she added.

Stevie volunteered to exercise him at least a few times.

"That's nice of you, but I know it'll be hard since you also have to work with Topside. You don't want to let him slip now that he's doing so well."

They discussed the other possibilities. Stevie agreed

87

that Lisa couldn't really do it. She *was* a good rider, but she didn't have the experience to handle Starlight if he continued being as moody as he had been. The minute he sensed any timidity on Lisa's part, he'd do exactly what he wanted.

"Who else? Let's see . . ." Stevie's voice trailed off as she thought.

"There is someone else, you know," Carole said hesitatingly. "Someone who's got a forced two-week vacation from riding."

"You can't mean Veronica!" Stevie cried, knowing that that was exactly who Carole meant.

Carole began cautiously. She knew how mad Stevie was at the suggestion, but she had to put Starlight first. "I know she tried to cause problems for you and Phil, but—"

"Cause problems! She tried to get him to dump me!"

"—and that's terrible, but she *is* a good rider." Carole paused, letting her words sink in. Then she added, "And I can't think of anyone at her level who won't be able to ride her own horse for two weeks. It seems like the best solution."

It was true. Carole couldn't ride at all. Veronica couldn't ride Garnet. And no matter how despicable Veronica was when it came to people, she *did* ride well. Even so, Stevie could barely bring herself to admit that Carole was right. She was still fuming inside over the phone call. "I guess it would be okay, but I'd think it over first," she said.

"I have, and it's the only sensible thing to do. I'll bet Lisa would think so, too," Carole said.

Stevie agreed that Lisa would like the logic of the situation. The horseless rider riding the riderless horse: It would work perfectly. "I guess so," she said.

Trying to cheer her up, Carole reminded Stevie that Starlight's well-being was at stake, and that that was all they should care about. Then she had to go—she wanted to soak her ankle before dinner. They finished the conversation and hung up.

Stevie knew that Carole's plan was the horsemanlike thing to do. Still, it filled her with disgust to think about The Saddle Club *again* doing something nice for Veronica. She would just have to keep her mind on her own plan—the plan of revenge!

CAROLE HAD BARELY got her Ace bandage off and her foot into the basin of warm water when the phone rang again. Colonel Hanson stretched the cord over to the kitchen table where Carole was sitting. Then he mumbled some excuse about having to do some desk work and left. Carole said hello eagerly, realizing it must be Cam. Her father would never excuse himself if one of her girlfriends called.

She was right: Cam's deep voice greeted her. Knowing

she could no longer keep her ankle a secret, she told him all about the trip to the hospital, ending with her plan to have Veronica ride Starlight. "What do you think?"

"Sounds fine," Cam muttered. Carole was puzzled. It was an unusual response for him. Normally he would be as eager as she was to weigh the pros and cons. Tonight he was answering everything she said in a monotone. He sounded distant and upset.

Carole decided to change the subject. Maybe he had had a bad day with Duffy and didn't want to talk horses. "So the party's still on, at least, and I think it'll be really fun."

There was a pause. "I guess you're inviting a lot of boys, huh?" Cam asked.

"I sure am," Carole said. "I want it to be as evenly numbered as possible."

"I hope I'm not ruining the ratio," Cam said.

"You?" Carole asked. What was that supposed to mean?

"Because if I am, I don't have to be there."

Carole was even more confused. Was this Cam's idea of a joke? He seemed to be asking her if she actually wanted him to come. "Cam, I want you there," she insisted.

When he didn't respond, she wondered if she'd said the right thing. Maybe *he* was the one who didn't want to come. Carole sighed. Why did people have to be so impossible to understand? Horses were so much simpler. She always knew what was bothering Starlight. She decided to drop the subject of the party and try yet another subject.

"Hey, did I tell you about what Veronica tried to do to Stevie and Phil?" she asked. She related the phone-call incident. "That's why Stevie doesn't want me to let Veronica ride Starlight. Can you believe Veronica would do something so awful? If Phil hadn't known better, she might have convinced him Stevie liked someone else."

Cam let out a long breath of air. "That's crazy," he said, sounding so relieved, he almost laughed. He warmed to the conversation right away. "From what I saw of her at the know-down, that sounds just like Veronica—dishonest and nasty. But I still think you're right to ask her to exercise Starlight. And if you want to spend time with him, you can always work him on the lunge line a little," he suggested.

Carole had no idea what she had said to cheer Cam up. In any case, he sounded like his old self. They chatted happily about the hayride. Neither of them could wait to see the Clydesdales. "We have to be very nice to Mr. Toll," Carole said. "My dad says he seems gruff because he talks less than Dapper and Dan, but actually he's just shy."

"The strong, silent type, huh? Just like me," Cam joked.

"That's not so far from the truth," Carole said. In fact, it was a part of Cam's personality she admired the most. He didn't talk all the time to make people notice him, but when he did, they respected what he said.

Cam mentioned that he would bring over a few CDs they could listen to at the party.

"I wish I could dance," Carole said. Even with games to play, she wasn't looking forward to sitting down all evening.

"You might not have to miss *all* the dancing," Cam said. "We might figure something out. I mean, you can always lean on me for support."

Carole smiled to herself. Cam holding her up beat crutches any day.

ON THURSDAY AFTERNOON after school Stevie and Lisa met at the mall with renewed determination. They were absolutely positive they could find the perfect gift—or at least a close second to the earrings.

"Either we find something today, or we buy her a book bag," Stevie said as they strode through the mall entrance.

"A book bag?" Lisa queried.

"My mother's suggestion. I figured if I mentioned it, it would give you even more incentive to find something here."

Lisa laughed. "Better than *my* mom's idea. She suggested a gift certificate for a manicure at the beauty shop." They giggled. The idea of Carole sitting in a salon while someone tried to clean the Pine Hollow dirt from under her nails was truly funny.

Once inside the main area of the mall, Stevie and Lisa could not decide where to go first. They decided to check the directory to get ideas. A group of kids their age were clustered around the placard that listed all of the shops. They stepped back to let Lisa and Stevie see.

"Shopping for Carole's gift?" a familiar voice asked. Stevie and Lisa turned to see Betsy Cavanaugh smiling at them. Once a Veronica-follower, Betsy had gotten nicer since she'd been dating James Spencer, a boy who took an occasional lesson at Pine Hollow. He was with her now, as were Helen and Tom Sanderson.

Stevie noticed that Betsy and James were holding hands—a good sign. It meant they were still going out and would come to the party together. "We're looking for a present for Carole, too," Betsy said.

"We already got ours," Helen said, trying to keep the smugness out of her voice but failing.

"The problem," Betsy said, "is that everyone knows it's going to be a great party, so everyone wants to bring the perfect gift instead of just trying to get something nice."

"What did you get, Helen?" Lisa asked.

Helen was happy to describe the present she and her brother were going to give Carole together. "Mom made both of us satin cross-country covers for our hard hats last year. We loved them so much, we asked her to do one for Carole in Pine Hollow colors, green and gray."

"So now we're just buying a card to go with it," Tom finished.

Everyone told them what a good idea it was. "I have to admit that it really is a superior present," Tom joked.

"So who's coming?" Helen wanted to know.

Lisa was about to answer when Stevie cut in. "We were about to ask you that," Stevie said. She elbowed Lisa. This would be the perfect opportunity to find out who liked whom.

"I know Adam Levine is coming," Helen volunteered. Stevie raised her eyebrows.

"I see," she said.

Helen glanced at her brother. "And, ahem, I also know that Meg Durham will be there."

"Oh?" Stevie said. Helen nodded.

Then Betsy shared her gossip. "In case you didn't know, Jen and Peter Schwartz are a couple again, and she invited him to go."

"Hmm . . ." Stevie said.

"And of course Polly and John."

"Of course," Stevie said. She was silent for a moment, frowning in concentration. Then she said, "So A.J. is going with Meg Roberts after all."

Betsy's jaw dropped. "Meg told me not to tell anyone. How'd you know?"

Stevie grinned. "Oh, just putting two and two together," she replied. "Come on, Lis—let's hit the shops."

The groups parted ways. Betsy and James headed for the pizza place to think. Helen and Tom headed for the stationery store at the end of the mall to look for cards. Stevie and Lisa found themselves walking toward The Saddlery.

"Are you going where I'm going?" Stevie asked.

"Where else are we going to find the perfect gift?" Lisa asked.

"Oh no!" Lisa exclaimed. She pointed. Just ahead of them Simon Atherton was walking by himself, whistling and swinging a shopping bag. His back was to them, and he hadn't seen them yet.

Stevie put a finger to her lips. She motioned for Lisa to turn around. "We can come back later," she mouthed. Lisa nodded vigorously. They did a swift turnabout.

"Lisa Atwood! Lisa and Stephanie!"

They stopped. "Hello, Simon," they said in unison. He came trotting up.

"Gosh, what a coincidence! Great to see you!" he said. "I'll bet you're shopping for Carole's present, huh? Well, I just found the perfect gift in The Saddlery. It's a little kit made of suede with scissors, a comb, a pull-through—everything you need for braiding a mane or tail."

As much as she wished they hadn't run into him, Lisa

couldn't lie to Simon: It was a wonderful gift, and Carole would love it. She told him so.

"Gee, gosh, I—I—" Simon turned red and stammered. "Hey, maybe I could help you look for your present," he volunteered eagerly.

Recalling her own pathetic state in the pizza parlor with Bob, Lisa took pity on Simon. "Okay," she said. "Thanks."

"Actually, we were just heading into The Saddlery," Stevie said. "But we forgot where it was," she added hastily when she saw a puzzled look cross Simon's face.

"Oh, I see. Well, it's right up here. Come on, I'll take you," Simon said proudly. They followed him into the store.

"Just our luck," Stevie murmured under her breath. Lisa followed her eyes to the counter. Veronica diAngelo stood there, paying for something at the cash register.

"At least she's buying Carole a present," Lisa whispered back.

"We'll see about that," Stevie said, sounding unconvinced.

"Gosh, it's Veronica! Hey, Veronica!" Simon called. Still completely oblivious to the tension between Veronica and The Saddle Club, he beckoned Lisa and Stevie over. "Can you believe it? Running into three friends in one day! Boy-oh-boy!" Simon grinned with pleasure.

Veronica gave him a big smile, looking right past Stevie and Lisa.

"Simon Atherton, fancy meeting you here," she said.

"I'll bet you're doing what we're doing," Simon guessed.

"Oh? Are you having your riding coat monogrammed, too?" Veronica asked.

Simon gave her a conspiratorial wink. "Ha, ha—very funny—I—"

Stevie cut in. "Actually, no. I personally don't think it's necessary to put my initials all over everything I own."

"Jealousy is so unbecoming," Veronica retorted.

Simon grinned. "Gosh, you girls are too funny—always pretending to fight. Now, come on, let's all look for Carole's present together."

Veronica's face darkened in anger. "Actually, I was just leaving." She spun on her heel to go and then paused for a moment. "I mean, don't you want to come with me, Simon? You promised to buy me an ice cream."

"I did?" Simon asked.

Veronica took his arm proprietorially and started to walk him out the door. "I'm so glad you remembered."

"So we'll meet up afterward, right?" he asked.

Veronica shot Lisa and Stevie a dirty look over her shoulder. "Oh, right," she said. "Naturally."

Before Stevie and Lisa could say anything, they were gone.

"Ever heard the expression 'killing two birds with one stone'?" Stevie asked.

Lisa laughed. "I think I just found out what it meant. Veronica actually thinks she and I are in a war over Simon, doesn't she?"

Stevie nodded. "Which is exactly what we're hoping she thinks."

"It's incredible that she hasn't realized what a nerd Simon is," Lisa said.

"She probably doesn't stop talking about herself long enough to find out," Stevie guessed.

Now, with both Simon and Veronica out of the way, they could finally turn to serious gift shopping. Shelf by shelf, they went over the merchandise in the tack shop.

"A jumping bat?" Lisa suggested. She picked up the short crop, used especially for stadium jumping.

"That's what Phil and A.J. are getting her," Stevie said. They both sighed.

"Why does everyone else have all the good ideas?" Lisa asked.

"I don't know, but I feel like we should come up with the *best* gift, because we're her best friends."

Lisa agreed. It felt important that they give Carole something really special. Inevitably, they found themselves wandering over to the counter where the jewelry was.

"We're only going to make ourselves miserable," Lisa said.

"I know," Stevie replied glumly. The earrings were in the same place as before, looking just as perfect—and just as expensive.

The gray-haired saleswoman came bustling over. "Now, what's that I hear? Why should looking at my nice jewelry make you miserable?" she asked.

"Because we found the perfect birthday gift for our friend," Lisa said.

The woman smiled kindly. "That doesn't sound miserable," she said.

"Yeah, well, it's those earrings, and we can't afford them," Stevie explained. She pointed to the gold horse-shoe earrings.

"They are a lovely pair, aren't they?" Stevie and Lisa nodded silently. "Now, let me see," the woman said. "I think I might be able to help." She opened and closed several tiny drawers underneath the counter. Finally she took out a small white jewelry box. She lifted the lid.

"Would these do, by any chance?" Stevie and Lisa peered inside the box intently.

"It's the same pair!" Stevie exclaimed.

"Only in silver!" Lisa cried.

"They're twenty-four ninety-five with tax," said the saleswoman.

Stevie let out a whoop. She hugged Lisa, and they danced around in front of the counter excitedly. "Yippee! The perfect gift! She'll love them!" Stevie shouted.

Not wanting to spoil the mood, Lisa asked quietly, "Do we have twenty-four ninety-five?" Stevie stopped dead in her tracks. Lisa whipped out her wallet from the little blue purse she carried. Stevie reached into her jeans pocket and drew out a fistful of bills and change. Lisa neatly stacked her money on the counter. Stevie poured her money on top. She watched as Lisa smoothed out the bills and counted aloud. "Ten, twenty, twenty-one, twenty-two, twenty-three, twenty-three fifty, twenty-three seventy-five, twenty-four—" Stevie looked anxiously at the remaining change. There was a dime and two nickels. They had $24.20.

"Wait a minute!" Stevie cried. She yanked off her sneaker and shook out a quarter. "Just in case I ever need it," she explained to the incredulous saleswoman.

"Twenty-four forty-five," Lisa said. "We need another fifty cents."

"Did I say twenty-four ninety-five?" the saleswoman asked with a twinkle in her eye. "I meant twenty-four forty-five."

Once again the girls whooped with delight—this time even more loudly than before. Lisa gathered up the money and presented it to the saleswoman ceremoniously. The woman took the money and the box to the cash register. Lisa felt a wave of gratitude when she noticed her slipping in two quarters from her own purse. Then, in a few neat motions, the woman gift wrapped the earrings in The Saddlery's distinctive horse-head wrapping paper. After she had been thanked about ten times by each of them, the saleswoman shooed them out the door.

"Have a nice party!" she called.

"We *will!*" Lisa and Stevie yelled. Now there was *another* reason to look forward to Saturday: They couldn't wait to see the look on Carole's face when she opened her present.

CAROLE SCRATCHED STARLIGHT'S neck as best she could. The only way she could get a hand free was to lean all her weight on her crutches, holding herself up by her underarms. Even after being groomed this way, Starlight was still suspicious of the bright, awkward-looking crutches. Whenever he caught sight of them, he snorted and swiveled his ears back and forth.

"I know, boy, but you might as well get used to them now," Carole told him. "Because you're going to be seeing them for two weeks." Starlight didn't seem to understand. He shifted uneasily on the cross-ties. He was all groomed now and ready for his saddle and bridle. But instead of putting them on, his owner was carrying two big sticks around.

"I can't ride today, Starlight," Carole explained. "Doctor's orders. I'm lame, just like Garnet." Carole gestured toward the next stall, where she could hear the mare pawing the floor impatiently. Starlight tossed his head in the closest thing to a human shrug Carole could imagine.

She scratched his neck some more, and when Garnet pawed again, she went over and gave the mare a pat. "This time there's a reason you're inside, Garnet. Poor thing—you don't know that. Probably bored out of your mind. Just like me—I'm grounded and you're shut in— we're a perfect pair." Starlight tossed his head again, this time to get Carole's attention. "I know, you're bored, too —only you're perfectly fine," she said, going back to him.

Seeing the two horses together reminded Carole of her idea to ask Veronica to ride Starlight. She knew it was the right thing to do. Here Starlight was getting restless after only his third day off—what would he be like after his second week? She decided to call the diAngelos' right away. The sooner Veronica could start, the better.

With a final pat she put Starlight back in his stall and went to use the phone in Mrs. Reg's office. She let it ring for a long time, but no one picked up. Mrs. Reg came into the room as Carole hung up the receiver. She motioned Carole over to her desk and told her to have a seat. "You look glummer than a cat in the rain. Is the ankle bothering you?" she asked.

"Not too much, now that I've got the bandage and crutches and everything. It's Starlight I'm worried about," Carole said.

"You don't think he'll like his two-week holiday?" Mrs. Reg asked.

"He might enjoy it, but by the time I get back on, he'll explode," Carole predicted. She explained her Veronica-Starlight plan to Mrs. Reg. The older woman thought it was a good idea.

"If I see Veronica, I could ask her for you," Mrs. Reg offered.

"Okay, thanks," Carole said. She thought for a minute. She really didn't want to rely on Mrs. Reg's being around when—and if—Veronica chose to make an appearance at Pine Hollow, but there didn't seem to be another way of getting in touch with her. The diAngelo line was permanently busy or there was no answer. Carole looked around Mrs. Reg's office idly, deciding what to do. Catching sight of a stack of notepaper on Mrs. Reg's desk, she remembered her original impulse—to leave a note on Garnet's stall. Besides, Veronica still hadn't RSVP'd about the party, despite the message Carole had left with the maid. By leaving a note, she could make doubly sure Veronica knew about the party and ask her to ride Starlight at the same time.

Carole borrowed a piece of paper and a pen from Mrs. Reg. She chewed on the end of the pen for a minute, then scribbled hastily, "*Hi, Veronica! Hope to see you Saturday at six for my birthday. Also, I hurt my ankle—any chance of your riding Starlight while Garnet's off?—Carole.*" Taking several strips of masking tape, she stuck the note in an envelope and secured it to the bolt on Garnet's stall door.

10

"HAVE FUN, DEAR!" Mrs. diAngelo waved a red-nailed hand out the Mercedes's window.

Veronica put her hands on her hips and sneered in disgust at her mother. "I'm supposed to have fun holding my lame horse while the vet looks at her?" she asked. "Yeah, real fun, *Mother.*"

"I'm sure you'll find a way to enjoy yourself," said Mrs. diAngelo airily.

Veronica gave her another dirty look. In response Mrs. diAngelo smiled wanly and drove off. "You'll regret saying that, Mother!" Veronica muttered. The very thought of having to come to Pine Hollow and not even ride was an outrage. Veronica wanted to punch someone or pull someone's hair. Instead she kicked some stones on the driveway. "Stupid stones. Stupid, stupid stones." She repeated the words all the way into the barn, scuffing her imported Italian loafers as hard as she could in the dirt.

Knowing she wasn't going to ride, Veronica hadn't even bothered to change from her school outfit. She was wearing a silk blouse underneath an off-white cashmere sweater with matching cream-colored pants. She carried a leather pocketbook that went with her shoes. They were all things her mother had picked out and given her a few days ago. By the time she reached the barn, they were completely covered in dust and barn grime. She stopped at the doors, yanked off her pale-pink-and-cream hair ribbon 'and threw it down into a puddle. Then she stepped on it, grinding it into the mud. "Hmph," she said aloud. "I *am* enjoying myself, after all."

A quick glance down the aisle revealed that Judy Barker had already arrived. As she had planned, Veronica was late. There was a good chance that Judy had found someone else to hold Garnet by now. Anyway, it was completely pointless for her to be there at all, Veronica thought. Judy could examine Garnet on cross-ties just as easily. But the vet had insisted that she come.

"What a waste of a day," Veronica mumbled, coming

up to Garnet's stall. The mare was standing in the aisle while Judy ran a hand down her foreleg.

"Oh, good, you're just in time to hold your horse," Judy said. "I'm glad I'm running late, too, or you would've missed me."

With a scowl Veronica took the lead line the vet handed her. "I've already checked her hoof, but you can take her out to the driveway and trot her for me," Judy said. Veronica was about to protest, but the look on Judy's face made her bite her tongue. She sluggishly walked the mare outside. Judy had her jog Garnet up and down the driveway several times. At least, Veronica noted with pleasure, her clothes were getting even filthier.

Finally Judy called her over. "Okay, put her away," she said.

"Well?" Veronica demanded.

"Well what?" Judy asked.

"Well, can I ride her or not?"

"Ride her? Oh, no. Definitely two weeks off."

Veronica glared at her.

"After that we'll have to see," Judy said with a smile. "Go ahead and take her in."

With ill-concealed irritation, Veronica said, "I'll do that, Judy. Thank you so much for your time."

As they were walking back in to Garnet's stall, Simon Atherton appeared at the entrance to the barn.

"Hey, have you seen Lisa anywhere?" he asked. "I've been looking all over."

Veronica glared at him impatiently. She wondered if her afternoon could get any worse. As if it weren't awful enough to have to deal with a lame horse, now The Saddle Club's geeky friend was bothering her about the annoying girl he had a crush on. She was almost *glad* she wasn't invited to the stupid party—she wouldn't have to see the two of them together.

Veronica was about to flash him one of her worst looks when all at once her brain caught up with her thoughts. The Saddle Club. A party she wasn't invited to. Lisa Atwood. Simon Atherton. Nobody at the barn but her. She smiled sweetly at Simon, inwardly congratulating herself on eavesdropping on Stevie's conversation with Bob Harris. She began surreptitiously to brush her clothes off and straighten her hair. "Simon," she said, "I hate to break this to you, but Lisa's probably hanging out with her friends at the mall. *Some* people just can't be bothered to take a genuine interest in horsemanship."

Judy interrupted Veronica's tirade. "Actually, Simon, I heard Max say something about Lisa and Stevie helping Carole decorate for her birthday party this afternoon."

Simon gaped. "Oh, wow, the party," he breathed. "I forgot. Gosh, too bad I missed them. I sure would have

109

loved to help out. It's going to be a great party. I mean, gosh, this is the first party I've ever been—"

"I guess *some* people will look for any excuse to get out of taking care of their horses," Veronica commented.

The three of them had reached Garnet's stall. Judy gave the mare an affectionate pat. Then, chuckling to herself, she hopped into her truck.

"Gosh, Veronica," Simon said. "I sure feel bad for you, being such a dedicated rider and all, and having your horse go lame."

"That's okay," Veronica said, visibly brightening. Maybe, she thought, the day wouldn't be such a loss after all. "Any good rider has a horse go lame once in a while. I'll just have to cope with it. It's hard, but I'll get through it. The horse always has to come first."

Veronica paused for a moment, listening to the sound of Judy's engine start. Then she said, "Of course, it would help if a person could get a decent veterinarian around here."

Simon's eyes widened. "You mean Dr. Barker's no good?" he asked.

Veronica put her face close up to Simon's. She whispered, "Just between you and me, she's been known to make her mistakes."

"Like what?"

"Oh, it's not important."

"Gosh, Carole thinks she's the greatest," Simon said, backing away. "You oughta put her straight."

"Yeah, maybe sometime," Veronica snapped. She took the lead line off Garnet's halter and closed the stall door. There was an envelope taped to the bolt. No doubt it was Judy's bill. "The nerve of that woman! She hardly did anything!" Veronica cried. She ripped the envelope off the door, crumpled it up, and shoved it into her pocketbook.

Simon persisted. "This is serious. What if she messed up on one of the horses here? Maybe you could tell Carole at the party. I'm sure she'd want to talk to Max."

"I, ah, don't think that would be a good time to bring it up."

"Why not? I know it's her birthday and all, but with Carole—I mean, with Carole *and* you—horses always come first, right?"

Veronica thought fast. She wasn't about to admit that she hadn't been invited to the party everyone was talking about. That would be just what The Saddle Club wanted—for her to humiliate herself in front of Lisa's date. "Oh, ah—I'm, um, I'm not going to be able to make the party, actually," she lied.

"Too bad," Simon said, his face falling. "It sure sounds fun."

Veronica looked up at him and smiled brightly.

"Maybe you'd prefer to spend the evening at my house. My mother and father would love to meet you. I've told them so much about you."

"You have?" Simon asked.

"Well, naturally. I always tell them about the boys I meet—if I like them, that is." Simon gulped. "Of course you might not want to come over—it's the cook's night off, so we'd probably have to ask the maid to make something for us, and it might not be up to your standards. . . ." She let her voice trail off.

"Gosh, Veronica, I would, but—"

"Oh, I understand. It's okay." She sniffed loudly. "It's just that I—I couldn't bring myself to go out to a party when I know that poor Garnet is locked up in her stall in pain. I just wouldn't be able to have a good time, knowing she was hurt. So I told Carole I couldn't go." She wiped her eyes and looked forlornly at the ground. "You probably think I'm silly," she said.

"Not at all," Simon said fervently. He looked at Veronica with new admiration. He had never known such a devoted rider. All thoughts of Lisa had fled his mind. Veronica seemed to like him as much as he liked her. If only there was something he could do to make her less upset. He had to help her. "Listen, Veronica, it might do you good to go out and forget about Garnet for a while," Simon suggested.

"Forget about her? My baby? How could I?" Veronica

buried her face in Garnet's mane. The mare laid her ears back.

"Don't be mad at me," Simon pleaded. "I just thought you might feel better if you came with me to the party."

Veronica looked up. "Came with you?" she asked, sniffling.

"Yeah, I mean, well—you could be my date. We could go together. I'll bet we'd have a lot of fun."

"But what about—you know . . ." Veronica decided not to mention Lisa by name. Maybe Simon didn't realize who he was *supposed* to be going with.

"Oh, that doesn't matter! Just because you told Carole to cross you off her list doesn't mean you can't go. I heard that there was plenty of room for kids to bring dates. So, see—you can go with me."

"I suppose I could," Veronica said, pretending reluctance. "I just don't know. I should probably sleep here Saturday, move a cot into Garnet's stall—"

"You don't have to go with me if you don't want to. It's okay," Simon said hastily.

"—but since you did ask, I'll go," Veronica finished.

"Great!" Simon fairly shouted. He could barely contain his excitement. He, Simon Atherton, had convinced a girl to forget about her life's work with horses and go to a party with him. "Let's shake on it," he said. He extended a hand.

Veronica took it. She couldn't explain Lisa's bad taste

in boyfriends. But Lisa's bad taste was Veronica's good luck. She was going to show up—uninvited—at Carole's stupid party, after all, and she'd be coming, not alone, but with Lisa Atwood's date, the boy the whole Saddle Club had picked out for her.

"SOMEBODY BETTER COME take these pizzas out of the oven!" Colonel Hanson hollered from the kitchen. His voice was barely audible over the din in the family room.

"Carole can't move right now!" Stevie called back. "But I'll be right there!"

"I'll help!" Phil volunteered.

Carole thanked them happily. She was sitting on the couch, wedged between Cam and Lisa, balancing a tray of nachos and salsa on her lap.

It was six-fifteen, and already the party was in full swing. Lisa, Stevie, Cam, Phil, and A.J. had all arrived early to help out with the last-minute preparations, and the doorbell hadn't stopped ringing since. Colonel Hanson had put everyone to work opening bags of pretzels and chips, bringing up soda from the basement, and retacking streamers that had fallen down.

Thanks to Lisa and Stevie's help the day before, the family room had been completely transformed. Streamers hung from every available surface. Bunches of balloons were tied to furniture and floating overhead. A huge computer printout tacked to the wall behind the couch read: Happy Birthday, Carole! Two card tables stood against one of the walls, one piled with colorfully wrapped presents, the other groaning with deliciously unhealthy food.

"What a ton of junk food," Stevie said, eyeing the refreshment table appreciatively. She and Phil added two pepperoni pizzas to the mass of snacks. "My mother would freak." Mrs. Lake, who believed in good nutrition, didn't let Stevie and her brothers eat sugar cereal—let alone caramel corn, chips, chocolate kisses, and mini candy bars.

"Oh, c'mon—it's not all junk food. There's that one plate of carrot sticks and celery," Phil pointed out.

"Yeah, and my mother brought them!" Stevie cried, grinning.

"Good thing Colonel Hanson's keeping her busy in the kitchen. She can't see what we're eating in here," Phil said. Some of the parents—including Mrs. Lake— were lingering in the kitchen to talk with each other.

Luckily, Colonel Hanson was making sure they didn't venture out to the living room and disrupt the festivities.

Carole looked around her. Even with her leg up on a footrest, it was a perfect party. She was completely comfortable. Cam was sitting on her left, chatting easily with Lisa. The Sandersons, John O'Brien, and Meg Durham were playing a "Pin-the-Tail-on-Starlight" game that Stevie and Phil had made as a joke. Betsy Cavanaugh was teaching another group of kids how to untie a human knot. Everyone else was talking or stuffing themselves with junk food—or both. Carole counted heads. The only people they were waiting for were Veronica, Simon Atherton, and Bob Harris. Since Veronica had never answered her invitation, and no one cared if Simon showed up or not, the only person they were *really* waiting for was Bob.

Carole stole a glance at Lisa. She was wearing the new blue sweater over corduroys with navy flats. Carole prayed that when and if he arrived, Bob would notice how well the sweater set off her fair complexion. Lisa seemed pleased to be talking with Cam, but Carole noticed that she kept glancing toward the door and looking at her watch. From across the room Stevie noticed, too. Carole gave her a meaningful glance.

"Come on, Lisa, why don't you help me bring up some more soda," she suggested.

"Good idea," Lisa said. She sounded relieved to have

something to do. The two of them disappeared down-stairs.

Cam took the opportunity to give Carole's hand a squeeze. "It's a great party, Carole. Everyone's having a good time—especially me," he said softly. He pulled her a little closer. "I—" Carole leaned in to catch his next words. "I, um—"

"Cam!" Colonel Hanson's deep bass boomed across the room. "You look like the man I need!"

"Yes, sir!" Cam said, jumping up.

In spite of herself, Carole burst out laughing. "I guess Dad really has that commanding tone of voice, huh? You jumped up like a private at inspection!"

Cam grinned. "I do aim to please, ma'am," he said. He gave Carole's hand another squeeze and went to see what Colonel Hanson wanted in the kitchen. Carole got to her feet, too. She wanted to talk to the rest of the kids for a while since she'd been sitting with Cam for almost half an hour.

The minute she stood up, the doorbell rang. "I'll get it!" she called, hobbling over to the door. She swung it open eagerly, hoping to see Bob Harris. Instead, Veronica and Simon Atherton stood on the doorstep. Carole was surprised to see the two of them arriving together. Moreover, the look on Veronica's face was pure gloat, and Carole had no idea why.

"Did you two carpool over?" she asked finally, after welcoming them inside.

Veronica looked offended. "Well, naturally," she replied. "I mean, since we were coming *together*, I of course had my chauffeur pick Simon up, too. I *suppose* you expected Simon to come *alone*."

It took Carole a moment to absorb this information. Then she realized that Veronica meant that Simon was her date and vice versa. She could hardly believe her ears. Veronica diAngelo—gloating over bringing the nerdiest, dorkiest guy The Saddle Club knew as her date? Something very strange was going on.

Remembering her duty as a hostess, Carole said, "I'm so glad you could both come." She wasn't sure what else to say. Veronica seemed so proud of the fact that she had shown up, one, with Simon, and two, without ever answering Carole's invitation.

Stevie and Lisa emerged from the basement staircase carrying plastic liters of soda. They set them down by the card tables. Noticing the group at the door, they immediately came over to rescue Carole from what looked like an awkward situation.

Veronica flashed the two of them a superior smile. "Why, Lisa—you decided to come, anyway. Of course, *Simon* and I didn't think you should stay home—in fact, I have to say that I admire you for being such a good sport."

Carole was about to ask Veronica what she meant when the doorbell rang again. She opened the door. This time a cute, blond, red-faced boy stood there. Carole knew it had to be Bob Harris.

She introduced herself and then said kiddingly, "Since I don't recognize you, you must be Bob Harris!"

"That's right," Bob said, "and a very late Bob Harris. I'm really sorry." While The Saddle Club plus Veronica and Simon listened, Bob explained that he had lost the address and—not wanting to look stupid—had looked up "Hanson" in the phone book. Unfortunately, he had picked the wrong Hanson. "So I ended up across town, knocking on some strangers' door, and insisting that they had a daughter named Carole who was having a birthday party!" Bob finished. The Saddle Club dissolved into good-natured giggles.

Simon began snorting and chuckling. "Gosh-oh gosh-oh gosh, that is the ultimate story, huh, Veronica?" He reached out and slapped her on the back.

Veronica's face froze in a pained expression. She was beginning to have a bad feeling about the party. "Hello, Bob. I didn't know you were going to be here," she said. Her voice sounded as if it was going to crack.

"Yes, Veronica, I'm here. I guess I'm not too *delicate* for a birthday party," Bob answered. Then he turned back to The Saddle Club. "Anyway, pleased to meet you and happy birthday, Carole, and again, I apologize," Bob said. He looked Lisa directly in the eye and asked, "Forgive me?"

"Anytime," Lisa said, her heart skipping a beat. She and Bob stared at each other for a minute.

"Ahem," Stevie said.

Remembering himself, Bob finally broke the silence. "Nice sweater. That color's great on you." Lisa blushed beet-red and mumbled thank you.

"Bob, I—" Veronica began.

"Yes?" Bob asked coldly.

Veronica swallowed. She looked from him to Lisa. Lisa was beaming, her eyes on Bob. "Nothing," Veronica said. "Absolutely nothing."

It was all Stevie could do to keep from laughing aloud and giving high fives all around. Her moment of triumph over Veronica had arrived, and she was looking forward to savoring the victory all evening. Deciding it was high time that she get back to the party—and as far away from Veronica as possible—Stevie began to shepherd Bob and Lisa back toward the others. "Come on, Bob," she said. "We've got to introduce you to everyone and get you in on some games."

Simon, who had been quiet during the exchange, all at once blurted out, "How 'bout a game of Simon Says, Stephanie? I'll be the leader, heh-heh." He doubled over with laughter at his own joke. Veronica glared at him with distaste. Everyone else smiled tolerantly.

"Uh, maybe later, Simon," Stevie said. She, Bob, and Lisa walked over to join the crowd, each of them grinning from ear to ear. Bob and Lisa were grinning at each other. Stevie was grinning at them but also to herself.

Joining Phil, she murmured, "Project Date-for-Lisa just ran head-on into Project Revenge-on-Veronica. And I, for one, like the results." Phil held out his hand for her to give him five. She did, loudly.

CAROLE TURNED TO Veronica. Simon had draped an arm over her shoulder, which Veronica was trying to shrug off. "What I was going to say was that I didn't know if you'd make it, since you never answered the invitation," Carole said.

Whatever was left of the smirk she'd had when she came in completely died on Veronica's face. She cleared her throat. "Invitation?" she asked faintly.

"Yes, I left the message with the maid because I couldn't get through on your line," Carole explained, growing annoyed. Did Veronica have to go on playing dumb? "The night I called everyone else, it was busy for over an hour."

Veronica attempted a fake smile but failed. "Message? With the maid? I never read anything she gives me," she said wanly. Veronica thought for a minute. All at once she realized what had happened. "Do you mean to tell me that I went to all this effort to—I mean—I tried to—" Veronica stopped, pouting. Her eyes flashed angrily. There was nothing she could say. She couldn't exactly complain about having been invited.

"At least you were able to come—with Simon," Carole said sweetly, beginning to understand the situation.

"Darn right, with me!" Simon said. "Why, gosh, Carole, this practically makes you a matchmaker! This party is almost as good as a petri dish—you know, those things you grow bacteria in. See, Veronica and me—we're like two pieces of bacteria . . ."

Veronica stared at him. She had an intense desire to tear his hair out and run screaming out the door. She looked away to calm herself. She saw Lisa and Bob sitting on the couch, sharing a piece of pizza. Phil and Stevie were sitting on the floor, arm-wrestling. All four looked completely happy together. Veronica caught Stevie's eye. Stevie looked at her and then—meaningfully—at the telephone. Veronica drew in a sharp breath and looked away hastily. Stevie knew about the phone call to Phil!

". . . and all the little bacterial *E. coli* keep growing and growing and—"

Carole broke into Simon's monologue. "What about the note I left on Garnet's stall door?" she asked Veronica.

With a sinking feeling Veronica groped around in her cream pocketbook and drew out the now crumpled note.

"This? Oh, I—uh—never looked at this, either," she said brusquely. "I mean, really, a note on a stall door."

"I wanted to be absolutely positive you got the invitation," Carole said, putting on her best hostess smile. She told Veronica its contents, including the part about her ankle and her hope that she, Veronica, would exercise Starlight while Garnet was lame. "It just seemed like the logical solution, don't you think?"

"Gosh, it sure seems superlogical to me," Simon said. Both Carole and Veronica gave him a withering look.

Not meeting Carole's eyes, Veronica said yes, she thought it was a good idea. She stared at the floor. How could she have known The Saddle Club would include her—even go out of their way to be friendly? She had totally misjudged them. She kept her eyes intently on the floor, wishing it would open up and swallow her. She looked up when she heard the sound of a male voice. Cam had come over to see how Carole was doing and to offer her a chair.

"Actually," Carole said, "I was about to come rescue you from my father. What's he got you doing now?"

"We've been moving stereo equipment, but it's a secret," Cam whispered. He put his arm lightly around Carole's shoulder to help her back to the sofa. She leaned on his strong frame.

Veronica stared after them.

Simon poked her in the ribs. "Cheer up, Ronnie, the party's just beginning," he said. Veronica glared at him.

"Lisa and Stevie, let's get the rest of the pizza, okay?" Carole beckoned her two friends to follow her. In about two seconds The Saddle Club had convened in the kitchen, leaving Bob, Cam, and Phil to get to know one another better. The parents had finally cleared out, so the room was empty.

Stevie thumped Carole on the back. "Gosh, swell party, Carole—almost as swell as my trigonometry course, where we're learning all about sine and cosine waves."

"All right, all right," Carole said, when the three of them had managed to stop giggling. "I think I know what happened, but somebody explain."

Stevie's face grew very solemn. She looked gravely at Lisa. "Lisa, I'm terribly sorry that Veronica has stolen the man of your dreams. But I guess you'll just have to settle for Bob Harris."

Lisa laughed. She looked excited and happy. "I can hardly believe Bob's here—and that your plan worked. Veronica came with Simon because she thought *I'd* be jealous!" she said.

"I see you've been busy plotting while I've been out of commission, huh, Stevie?" Carole asked.

"It was Lisa's idea!" Stevie protested. "Remember when she said that if we were lucky, Veronica and Simon would entertain each other? Well, I just decided I'd make sure. Luckily, Veronica cooperated perfectly. She figured Simon Atherton was her chance to get back at The Saddle Club—"

"For not inviting her to the party!" Carole cried, now fully understanding. "She never got either of my invitations. She just wanted to crash a party she wasn't invited to—with a stolen date!"

Stevie shook her head. "All that scheming for nothing. She's probably disappointed that she *was* invited!"

Carole had to agree. "Knowing Veronica, she probably is."

Stevie leaned back into the cushions and groaned. "Oh, my aching stomach. I can't eat another bite," she pronounced to the group gathered around the couch.

Phil smiled at her wickedly. "Not even another chip? One more nacho? How 'bout a carrot stick?" he asked, waving the plate under her nose. Stevie groaned again. "A soda?" Phil offered.

"I'm never eating again as long as I live, Phil Marsten," Stevie said.

Carole, sitting with Cam on the rug, reminded her with a grin, "Don't forget—there's still cake and ice cream when we come back."

"Okay," Stevie said. "I'm never eating again until the cake and ice cream," she decided. Everyone laughed.

"Come back from where?" A.J. asked.

Carole was about to respond, but Cam put his finger to his lips. "Listen," he said. Everyone quieted down and strained their ears toward the door. There was a jingle of bells, and then a man's voice cried out, "Whoa, Dapper —whoa, Dan. Easy does it!"

"If I didn't know better, I'd say it was Santa Claus arriving a month early," remarked Bob Harris. Everyone laughed again. They were all in such good moods that anything anyone said seemed to be incredibly funny. Lisa laughed particularly hard.

"Actually, Bob, you're practically right," Carole said. "If anyone looks like Santa Claus, it's Mr. Toll. But I think that at seventeen hands, Dapper and Dan are a little bigger than the average reindeer."

"The hayride! I was having so much fun, I forgot!" A.J. cried.

They could have stayed there forever laughing and joking, but Carole was thinking of the horses. She didn't want them to get impatient. She called everyone to attention. "All right, gang. Let's get our coats and move out. *Nobody* keeps Mr. Toll waiting."

Colonel Hanson had had the same idea. He brought a pile of coats into the family room and began handing them out. In no time at all everyone was bundled up and trooping out the door, talking excitedly.

At the sight of the hay wagon, the group chatter

128

turned into *ooh*'s and *ah*'s. It was truly a beautiful scene. The huge wagon was piled high with hay bales. It had been freshly painted and gleamed in the dusk. The matched pair of bay Clydesdales stood calmly, champing on their bits and nosing each other every so often. Their powerful muscles shone with good care. As a special touch, someone had braided colorful yarn into their manes. Mr. Toll sat in the driver's seat, holding the traces and looking off into the distance.

"He looks like he's right out of the movies," Lisa whispered to Bob.

"I'm so glad he's real," Bob said.

Clad in denim overalls and a plaid wool work shirt with a straw hat atop his head, Mr. Toll did look like a Hollywood version of the country farmer.

Carole was completely taken aback by the horses. Lost in wonder, she gazed at their gorgeous coats and their noble, liquid eyes. "Let's go say hi," Cam said, reading her thoughts. He helped her over to the wagon. Carole reached out and patted one of the horses.

"Is this Dapper or Dan?" she asked timidly. She wasn't shy around the horses—it was Mr. Toll who made her feel awkward. He looked so stern!

"That's Dan. Dapper's a hand higher."

"They're so evenly matched. Are they related?" she asked.

Mr. Toll turned to look at her. He seemed surprised—

but pleased—at her interest in the horses. "Full brothers. Had their mother for twenty-six years. Finest Clydesdale brood mare in the state."

"I'll bet, with such beautiful offspring," Cam put in.

Mr. Toll nodded. "Ayup," he said. Carole could see the glint of pride in his eyes.

"The yarn looks lovely," she said.

"My wife did that."

"Thank you so much for taking us today."

"No need to thank me now. Haven't done anything yet," Mr. Toll answered curtly.

Carole was at a loss for words for a moment. Then she decided the military treatment would work well. "All right, sir, I'll thank you at the end, then." She and Cam gave Dapper and Dan a few more pats before going to climb onto the wagon. While they'd been talking, the rest of the party had jumped on and were getting settled to go.

"Hey, wait a minute, miss," Mr. Toll called. He picked up a stack of blankets from beside him. "Brought these— case it's cold," he said gruffly. He handed them to Cam.

Carole opened her mouth to say thank you. "Th—" Cam nudged her. She clamped her mouth shut. All thank-yous would have to wait till the end of the ride.

Cam helped Carole up into the wagon, then climbed up himself.

"Here, you guys!" Stevie cried. "We saved you a

bale!" She paused midthrow to gesture to Carole. Then she went back to attacking Phil and A.J. with handfuls of hay.

Once everyone had found a place to perch or sit—and Stevie and the boys had called a truce—Carole gave Mr. Toll the go-ahead.

"Not so fast!" Colonel Hanson yelled. He had been standing in the doorway, eagerly watching the proceedings. "You don't think I'm going to miss getting a shot of this for the album, do you?" He held his camera up to his face. "Okay, everyone smile—and look like you mean it!" he ordered.

"That's easy to do—I feel like my lips are set in a permanent smile, Colonel Hanson," Phil called.

"All right, then—one, two, three!" He snapped the shot, gave Mr. Toll the thumbs-up, and waved. Carole had asked her father earlier to join them on the hayride, but he had refused, saying he had stuff to do at the house. She couldn't imagine what, but had a hunch it just might have something to do with her birthday. She waved back just as Mr. Toll clicked his teeth and slapped the traces on Dapper's and Dan's backs.

Everyone gave a big cheer as the horses set off down the country road. The long-awaited hayride had begun!

LOOKING AROUND AT the animated faces of her friends, Carole had to smile. It was funny—all week long she and Stevie and Lisa had been thinking of almost nothing except who was going to sit next to whom, and who was dating whom, and who was going to smooch with whom during the course of the hayride. It wasn't turning out like that at all. Instead it was turning out to be a big bunch of friends having more fun than they could have imagined as they were pulled through town by a horse-drawn hay wagon. People stood or sat in groups of three and four, sometimes with their dates for the evening but other times not. Anyway, Carole thought, looking at the stiff back of their driver, no one in their right mind would risk being caught kissing by Mr. Toll!

Stevie caught Carole's glance and smiled back. The laughter and happy chatter were infectious. Stevie wanted to shout aloud for sheer joy. There was nothing like being one of twenty kids who were all having a wonderful time. Check that, Stevie thought, eyeing Veronica and Simon, make that nineteen kids having a wonderful time. Having won Simon's heart, Veronica could not shake him. He seemed to have decided that the hayride would be the perfect opportunity to tell her finally all about his hobbies. He had finished the growth and development of *E. coli* bacteria and moved on to stamp collecting.

As far as Stevie could tell, stamp collecting was not one of Veronica's great interests. Seeing the expression on Veronica's face, Stevie whispered to Lisa, "Looks like

132

Simon Atherton is so boring, he can even make something as incredibly exciting as stamp collecting sound dull."

Lisa looked over at the pair and had to stifle a chuckle. They really were a match made in heaven—with a little assistance from Stevie Lake.

"So then I saw the exceedingly rare double-eagle at an exhibition, but, alas, I was sidetracked by a beautiful collection from the Philippines, which ironically turned out to be worth less than a pair of sweaty gym socks because all the stamps had been canceled. You're probably wondering whether—"

While Simon droned on, the rest of the group had begun to sing camp songs. Helen and Tom Sanderson, known for their beautiful singing voices, were leading everyone in "I've Been Working on the Railroad." Veronica looked around unhappily. For once she found herself wishing she could join the group.

"—while, on the other hand, the Stamp Act of the eighteenth century had nothing to do with—"

In desperation Veronica opened her mouth wide and yawned loudly in Simon's face. To her dismay Simon yawned back happily. "Gosh, that's pretty funny, huh, Ronnie, how yawns are contagious. Of course, the lack of oxygen, which triggers the response of opening the mouth, can't scientifically be explained by—"

Veronica regarded Simon with revulsion.

* * *

THE EVENING HAD turned into a perfect night. The rays of the half-moon shone down, helping the pale orange streetlamps illuminate the night. The first stars had just appeared over the horizon and were glowing brilliantly.

One by one the group sang through all the popular songs they knew. Their voices rang out into the cool night air. The horses' steady walk was like a metronome ticking to keep the rhythm steady. Neighbors came out and stood on their doorsteps when they heard the singing. Some waved or joined in until the wagon had gone by. Mr. Toll doffed his hat as they passed. When it got too chilly, they stopped singing. Everyone bunched together and burrowed under the hay to keep warm. Lisa handed out the wool blankets that Mr. Toll had provided.

When they had scrunched down, A.J. insisted on telling a couple of ghost stories. Having lived through a *real* ghost story at their friend Kate Devine's ranch, The Saddle Club felt quite superior listening to the muffled shrieks around them. In case anyone was getting too scared, however, Carole told A.J. to think of something new. "And quit shining that flashlight under your chin," she said.

A.J. wailed good-naturedly, "Aw, I was just getting going! I haven't even gotten to the part about the rusty chain!"

Cam came to Carole's rescue. He suggested they play a memory game with the letters of the alphabet. "I'll start. It goes like this: My mother packed my trunk for camp, and she put in . . . an apple."

"Oh, I know that one," Betsy Cavanaugh piped up. "We used to play this on car trips. My mother packed my trunk for camp, and she put in an apple and . . . a birthday cake." The other kids caught on quickly, chiming in on the different letters. The game got hysterical because no one could seem to remember past H or J.

When they finally made it most of the way through the alphabet, Stevie jumped up. "All right, I'm warm— enough of this quiet fun. It's time for the final round of 'Smother the boys in hay'! Ladies, arm yourselves!" The boys put up a halfhearted protest but, for the most part, let themselves be smothered.

Before she knew it, Carole recognized the houses on her street. "We're almost home," she announced regretfully.

"Okay, one more song!" Tom Sanderson cried out. "And that's 'Happy Birthday'!" Everyone joined in, except for Carole, who sat on her hay bale beaming. All too soon the wagon had pulled up next to her house. Veronica jumped up like a bullet and ran to the front door. Simon panted after her. Other kids tumbled out of the back happily, stopping to thank Mr. Toll and pat the Clydesdales before going inside to the warm house. Carole got out last. She stepped carefully, once again helped by Cam's strong arms as support.

Together they said good-bye to Mr. Toll. This time he accepted Carole's thanks. "Anytime, miss," he said. Then he added gruffly, "That's as nice a bunch as we've ever taken, eh, Dapper and Dan?" He slapped the traces on their backs and set off toward home.

As they watched him go, Cam gave Carole a hug. "It was perfect, wasn't it?" Carole asked.

"And it's not over yet, birthday girl," Cam replied. Carole took the hand he offered and followed him into the house.

As soon as they came back in, Carole knew what her father had been up to during the hayride. He had converted the family room into a disco in their absence. The stereo had been moved from the living room to the stand where the TV usually sat. The lights were dimmed, and the rug that normally covered the wood floor had been rolled up and stood in a corner. There was even a mirrored disco ball flashing specks on the walls.

"Oh, Dad!" Carole cried out.

"Surprise, honey," Colonel Hanson said. "I borrowed the ball from the Officers' Club on base. Now get that stereo going! You're the disc jockey at Club Hanson tonight, and I want to see that floor packed with dancers."

He led Carole over to the stereo. In front of it he had placed his leather desk chair and footstool. There was a stack of CDs on the TV table. Some belonged to the Hansons, and others had been brought by Carole's friends.

Carole surveyed the music. She seized one of Cam's discs off the top. "You want dancers? This'll bring 'em out!" She put it in the CD player, turned up the volume, and waited to see what would happen.

"The Electric Slide! I love this!" Meg Roberts exclaimed.

"Me, too!" said Meg Durham. They jumped up, grabbing Bob, Lisa, Peter Schwartz, and Adam Levine. "Come on, we'll teach you!" Meg Roberts said.

Carole smiled contentedly. Sure enough, in a matter of minutes the couches and chairs were completely vacated, and almost everyone was at least making an attempt to learn the dance. Even Veronica had gotten up —and was dancing as far away from Simon as she could.

When the song ended, Carole had another fast song ready to go, to keep up the momentum of the party. Cam was sitting beside her, helping sift through the discs. Carole didn't want him to miss out on the fun. Just because she was stuck sitting didn't mean he had to sit, too.

"Hey, you should be out there dancing," she said. Cam shook his head.

"Really, I mean it," Carole said. She was about to tell him that he could go ahead and dance with anyone he wanted—except Veronica; but then she glanced out at the "dance floor." No one was dancing as pairs, anyway. The Electric Slide had set the tone for the evening. The whole party was dancing as a group and having a blast. They had made a huge circle, and every so often Phil or Stevie would call someone into the middle to do a solo. At the moment, John O'Brien was doing his imitation of a rapper while everyone cheered.

Simon Atherton was the only one who didn't seem to get it. He kept trying to break out of the circle and dance over to Veronica. She, meanwhile, was holding on to James Spencer and Tom Sanderson as tightly as she possibly could.

Cam and Carole watched the scene together, laughing. Satisfied that he was having a good time with her, Carole turned back to the job of music selection. "Hmmm . . ." she wondered aloud. "What next?"

Stevie danced over to the stereo. "Carole! Play some fifties music. Your dad and I are going to show everyone the Stroll and the Handjive!"

Carole laughed. Trust Stevie—who loved everything about the fifties—even to know the dances. She asked Cam to hand her Colonel Hanson's "Greatest Hits from the Fifties." Then they settled back to watch the fun. Stevie was really good. She could match Colonel Hanson motion for motion. Pretty soon everyone tried. Then, to keep them on their toes, Carole switched to "YMCA." Shouts of recognition and more enthusiastic dancing followed.

After a few more songs, Colonel Hanson interrupted, telling Carole he wanted to say something. He slowly faded the music out. "Okay, boys." He nodded toward Phil and A.J., who picked up the table of presents. They brought it over to Carole ceremoniously and bowed to her. The other kids gathered in a group around her—all except for Veronica, who excused herself and went to the bathroom.

"I guess I'm supposed to open these, huh?" Carole asked. She began to unwrap the first package Colonel Hanson handed her, gingerly removing the paper from the box.

"Come on, Carole Hanson! You can do better than that!" Stevie yelled.

Carole grinned. "You're right," she said. In one motion she tore off all the paper and ribbons. Inside was the satin cross-country hat cover from the Sandersons. "I love it!" Carole breathed. She held it up for everyone to see. For the next twenty minutes Carole said the same thing about every gift she opened—and meant it. Her friends had been so thoughtful in picking things out. For horsey gifts she got the jumping bat from Phil and A.J., the braiding kit from Simon, a pair of silk glove-liners, a calendar of the United States Equestrian Team, a package of premade horse treats, and two posters, one of racing Thoroughbreds, the other of a mare and foal. Her nonhorsey gifts were nice, too. There was some special German chocolate, a bunch of hair scrunchies, a mug with bubble bath in it, and a matching red scarf-and-gloves set. Carole felt as if she had said thank you a hundred million times, and there were still four gifts to go.

One was just an envelope. Carole opened it carefully. Two pieces of paper fell out. The first was a note. It said, *"Sorry we couldn't be there for the party. We're thinking of you, anyway. Love, Max and Mrs. Reg."*

"It's from Max and Mrs. Reg," Carole cried excitedly.

"They wanted to stop by tonight, but Mrs. Reg had to be in the city," Colonel Hanson explained. "So they dropped that off this morning when you were still asleep."

"What is it, anyway?" Lisa asked.

Carole looked at the other piece of paper. "It's a gift certificate for ice-cream sundaes at TD's!" she said. Then she quickly went on to her next present. Only Lisa, Stevie, and Carole knew exactly how perfect the gift certificate was, and none of them would want anyone else to feel left out.

The third-to-last gift was from Cam. Carole could easily recognize the handwriting on the card. She could also tell what the gift was going to be—it felt unmistakably like a book. She opened it carefully. The paper fell away, and the title jumped out: *Training the Young Horse for Pleasure and Show* by Gordon Morse. It was the book Cam had been telling her about! Carole opened the cover. Inside Cam had written, *"To the smartest rider and trainer I know—and the nicest."* Carole didn't trust herself to speak. Instead, she just looked at Cam with shining eyes. Cam looked right back, just as intently.

Gently, Colonel Hanson nudged Carole back to reality. "Two more to go," he whispered. Carole snapped back to attention. Of the two boxes left, one was medium-sized and flat, and the other was tiny and square.

"Go for the bigger one!" Phil urged. Stevie elbowed him. Phil laughed. "Whoops," he said.

Carole took his advice. She tore off the paper, almost losing the little card attached. Quickly, she read it aloud: " *'To Carole, Love, Dad'*—typical, gushy Hanson style, huh, Dad?"

Colonel Hanson chuckled, his eyes merry. "It says it all, right?"

Carole opened the box. "It's me!" she blurted out. Inside was a framed eight-by-ten color picture of her and Starlight soaring over the double oxer on Pine Hollow's outside course.

Carole reached over to hug her father. "I can't wait to

put it on my dresser," she said. "But where on earth did you get this, Dad?"

"I took it last summer—one day when I came early to pick you up," Colonel Hanson explained.

"We want to see!" the two Megs clamored. Carole passed the picture.

"Starlight looks perfect!" A.J. cried.

"So does Carole!" said Meg Durham reprovingly. Carole blushed. Even she knew how great a picture it was. Meg and A.J. were both right: The picture had captured one of those rare moments when both horse and rider were exhibiting near-perfect form. Starlight's knees were up and even, his ears were pricked, and his back was round, as he easily cleared the fence. Carole had released the reins correctly, and her knuckles were pressed firmly into Starlight's crest. Her position was tight and work-manlike. They looked as if they could jump six feet, let alone three.

"Want to come take my picture sometime, Colonel Hanson?" A.J. asked playfully.

"Yeah, maybe you should quit the Marines and become a show photographer," Helen joked.

"Beginner's luck," Colonel Hanson confessed.

By this point Lisa and Stevie were going out of their minds. They had watched patiently as Carole opened gift after gift without coming to the little box. Finally there was nothing else left. She *had* to open it. They looked at each other and crossed their fingers.

"Oh, I almost forgot. This last one," Carole said. She looked at the box and laughed. It had to be the fourth or fifth box she had received with the special Saddlery wrapping paper on it. Evidently, when it came to shopping for Carole, *everyone* knew where to go. She unwrapped it and lifted the little lid. The silver horseshoe earrings lay on the tissue, glowing like stars. They were absolutely beautiful. She didn't even have to ask who had brought them. No one else could have chosen such a perfect gift. She looked up and smiled at Lisa and Stevie.

AFTER THE FINAL crumb of cake had disappeared, it was time for the party to end. Carole picked out a last disc and put on a slow song. She grabbed her crutches and followed Cam out onto the dance floor. Half-leaning on the crutches, and half-leaning on Cam, she could sort of dance. Other couples followed their example. Phil and Stevie, then Lisa and Bob, Betsy and James, and then the rest of the group joined Carole and Cam on the dance floor. Over Cam's shoulder Carole smiled at the other girls. They all looked as happy as she felt. All of them, that is, except for Veronica. Having finally returned from the bathroom, she had found an all-too-eager Simon, waiting to slow-dance with his date. Veronica kept trying to pull away and pretend it was a fast song, but this time there was no one to help her.

Cam heard Simon say, "Gosh, I know my hands are a *little* sweaty, but I'll wipe them on my pants, Veronica, I promise."

He almost felt a touch of pity for Veronica—almost. Then he remembered the phone call. It was a good thing Phil had figured out who had called him about Stevie's "flirting" with Bob. Otherwise Cam might not have figured out *his* mysterious call. And he'd still be mad at Carole, for no reason other than Veronica's interference. All thoughts of pity left him. Holding Carole a little tighter, he smiled happily as Simon chased Veronica out into the hall.

Carole sighed as the song came to a close. She didn't want to lift her head from Cam's shoulder. His strong arms encircled her protectively, making her feel safe and warm. Dancing with him was one of the very best birthday presents she could have asked for. It was almost as good as watching Veronica get what she deserved. Carole sighed again. She could pretend the song—and her birthday—were still going for a couple more minutes.

COLONEL HANSON RAPPED lightly on Carole's bedroom door. "Anyone for pancakes?" he whispered. Three bodies in sleeping bags on the floor stirred slightly.

"What time is it?" Stevie asked hoarsely. She, Lisa, and Carole had been up most of the night rehashing the events of the day before.

"Eleven-thirty," Colonel Hanson said.

"In the morning?" Lisa asked, struggling to sit up.

"That's right," Colonel Hanson said with a chuckle. "And I have a feeling it might take you three a little while to make it downstairs, so I'll keep everything hot." He closed the door gently.

"Thanks, Dad," Carole called after him, wondering if she was still dreaming or if that had really been her father. She rubbed her eyes. Beside her Stevie and Lisa had lain back down in their sleeping bags. Then Carole remembered. "I insisted on sleeping on the floor with you guys, didn't I?"

"Actually," Lisa said, with her eyes still closed, "you didn't have much choice, considering that you fell asleep midsentence."

"Oh, yeah?" Carole countered. "What sentence was that?"

"It was, 'And the hundredth reason Cam is so perfect is that—' "

Carole interrupted her friend by whacking her soundly with a pillow.

"Funny," Carole said, "I remember hearing about the *thousandth* reason that Bob Harris is the ideal boyfriend."

Stevie sat up again. "You're both wrong. I mean, we all *know* that there are a *million* reasons why Phil Marsten is—" Before she could finish, both Lisa and Carole had pounced, and an all-out pillow–sleeping bag–blanket war erupted.

A few minutes later the three girls lay back, happy and winded. "I didn't know I had that much energy left," Lisa said.

"Me either. How late *did* we go to sleep?" Stevie questioned.

Carole grimaced. "Don't ask. Your parents might have to sue my father if they found out."

"Oh, Colonel Hanson's in the clear. He did tell us to stop talking five or six times. It's just that we outlasted him," Lisa said.

"I guess that's why he's up now, making pancakes for us," Carole said. "He did say something about pancakes, didn't he?"

Lisa and Stevie assured her that breakfast was awaiting them. Carole thought back to a week ago when she'd been eating pancakes with her father. It had been one of the fullest weeks she'd had in a long time. First, the sprained ankle—and her silly decision to pretend it didn't hurt. But then the party had come and simply made her forget about everything else except having a wonderful time. Every moment of it had been special, from decorating with The Saddle Club to dancing with Cam. It was impossible to say what part was the best!

"So are you going to see him again?" Carole heard Stevie ask Lisa as she tuned back in to the conversation.

Lisa nodded. "He's even nicer than I imagined. He mentioned something about the six of us maybe doing something."

"Of course!" Stevie cried. "A triple date! And now that Bob, Phil, and Cam are practically best friends, thanks to the party, it'll be perfect. It sure was a great party, Carole," she continued. "I guess my favorite part was when Veronica and Simon ran into your father as they were running into the hall. He told them to get right back into the family room. I think he probably thought they were trying to sneak off and make out!"

Lisa giggled. "If he only knew how hard Veronica was trying to *escape* Simon."

"You know she didn't even get me a present?" Carole remarked. "She hid in the bathroom the whole time I was opening them."

"She probably thought you'd have kicked her out by the time you got to opening the presents," Lisa guessed.

"But instead she had to spend the whole night with her charming date," Stevie pointed out cheerfully. "Okay, girls, let's get up."

Slowly The Saddle Club rose from the floor of Carole's bedroom. They looked at themselves in the mirror and laughed. Their hair was going every which way, and they all had circles under their eyes.

"So much for beauty rest," Lisa said. "We look scarier than Veronica when she found out she *was* invited." Laughing, the three of them began to straighten up the room and look for their clothes.

"You know," Carole said seriously, pulling on an acceptably clean pair of jeans, "we really owe one to Phil for noticing right off who it was who called him. Cam told me last night all about Veronica's plans to break *us* up."

"I guess that's just one *more* reason why Phil is the best boyfriend in the world, huh?" Stevie joked.

Carole smiled. "One more comment like that, and we may have to fix you up with Simon Atherton, eh, Lisa?"

"But you wouldn't want to try to break up him and Veronica," Stevie pointed out. "Veronica really deserves Simon."

"I'm sorry I ever invited her," Carole said. "And I'm even sorrier I ever asked her to exercise Starlight. After all that, Max told Dad that Red's been *hoping* I'd *let* him ride Starlight—he likes him so much. Of course, the reason I didn't want to ask him in the first place was that I didn't want to be like Veronica. Anyway, *she'll* never lay a finger on him now," Carole vowed.

"Phew," Stevie sighed. "I was getting worried for a minute that you'd gone over to *her* side."

"Hardly. I just wish I could take back being nice to her," Carole said.

"Don't worry about it," Stevie said. "Almost the worst punishment that Veronica could receive is being treated well by one of us."

"Stevie's right," Lisa chimed in. "It probably made her feel like a worm—and nothing should give us more pleasure than having Veronica diAngelo feel like a worm."

Carole nodded in agreement with her friends. "True," she said. She paused a moment. "Unless it's watching Veronica diAngelo have another date with Simon Atherton," she added.

"Gosh darn it!" Stevie cried. "You're right!"

ABOUT THE AUTHOR

BONNIE BRYANT is the author of more than sixty books for young readers, including novelizations of movie hits such as *Teenage Mutant Ninja Turtles®* and *Honey, I Blew Up the Kid*, written under her married name, B.B. Hiller.

Bonnie Bryant began writing The Saddle Club in 1986. Although she had done some riding before that, she intensified her studies then and found herself learning right along with her characters Stevie, Carole, and Lisa. She claims that they are all much better riders than she is.

Bonnie Bryant was born and raised in New York City. She lives in Greenwich Village with her two sons.

Saddle Up For Fun!

Join The Saddle Club

As an official Saddle Club member you'll get:

- *Saddle Club newsletter*
- *Saddle Club membership card*
- *Saddle Club bookmark*
- *and exciting updates on everything that's happening with your favorite series.*

Just fill out the coupon below and return by December 31, 1993 to:

Bantam Doubleday Dell Books for Young Readers
Saddle Club Membership Box BK
1540 Broadway
New York, NY 10036

SKYLARK

Bantam Doubleday Dell
Books for Young Readers

Name _____

Address _____

City _____ State _____ Zip _____

Age _____

Offer good while supplies last.

BFYR - 8/93